P9-DXI-368

THE
COLOR
OF FEAR

THE
COLOR
OF FEAR

Marcia Muller

GRAND CENTRAL
PUBLISHING

NEW YORK   BOSTON

This book is a work of fiction. Names, characters, places, and incidents are the product of the author's imagination or are used fictitiously. Any resemblance to actual events, locales, or persons, living or dead, is coincidental.

Copyright © 2017 by Pronzini-Muller Family Trust

Cover design by Blanca Aulet
Cover photograph by yunjun/Shutterstock
Cover copyright © 2017 by Hachette Book Group, Inc.

Hachette Book Group supports the right to free expression and the value of copyright. The purpose of copyright is to encourage writers and artists to produce the creative works that enrich our culture.

The scanning, uploading, and distribution of this book without permission is a theft of the author's intellectual property. If you would like permission to use material from the book (other than for review purposes), please contact permissions@hbgusa.com. Thank you for your support of the author's rights.

Grand Central Publishing
Hachette Book Group
1290 Avenue of the Americas, New York, NY 10104
grandcentralpublishing.com
twitter.com/grandcentralpub

First Edition: August 2017

Grand Central Publishing is a division of Hachette Book Group, Inc. The Grand Central Publishing name and logo is a trademark of Hachette Book Group, Inc.

The publisher is not responsible for websites (or their content) that are not owned by the publisher.

The Hachette Speakers Bureau provides a wide range of authors for speaking events. To find out more, go to www.hachettespeakersbureau.com or call (866) 376-6591.

Library of Congress Control Number: 2017942515

ISBN: 978-1-4555-3892-8 (hardcover), 978-1-4555-3891-1 (ebook)

Printed in the United States of America

LSC-C

10   9   8   7   6   5   4   3   2   1

For Bill, who knows all the reasons why

And in loving memory of my sister,
Carol Brandt

THE
COLOR
OF FEAR

TUESDAY, DECEMBER 19

2:47 a.m.

The old man stands at one of the display windows of a jewelry store in San Francisco's exclusive Marina district. He is tall and muscular, his face nut brown and deeply furrowed, and his long gray hair is tied back in a ponytail under his knit cap, falling over the collar of his flannel shirt. His jeans are faded but clean; his athletic shoes are scuffed, well used.

It is late, but he is not tired; with every advancing year he requires less and less sleep, as if his body is greedy to soak up every bit of life remaining to it. If even a few moments of that time should measure up to his earlier years, he will be rich in the experiences he treasures.

He has traveled here to San Francisco from his home on the Flathead Indian Reservation in Montana to spend the Christmas holidays with his daughter and her husband. San Francisco is not a city he has visited often, although the few times he did, he was impressed with it. For a number of years—long ago—he lived in New York City, which was necessary for his work. Then a young man, he had delighted in Manhattan's brashness and energy, but when he returned to the reserve in Montana its serenity had comforted him. Now he is intrigued by this California city that seems to be so many different things to such a diverse population.

Tonight he has gone out for his customary walk and is contemplating a Christmas gift for his daughter. Those aquamarine earrings displayed in the window would please her, complement her black hair and dark eyes. Color is of primary importance to him, an artist of some renown.

His daughter is also a gift—to him. The child he never knew he had until she sought him out a few years ago at his small home in St. Ignatius on the rez. "I need to trace my family's roots," she'd told him. "I need to know who I am."

At first he had been gruff with her, sent her away with orders to assemble her thoughts. His standard response when actually he'd needed to assemble *his*. But then she'd returned, and when all the twists and turns of their complicated lives had been sorted out, they had realized they were father and daughter. Of course, mere blood ties are less than what is required to forge a true relationship. But they'd worked at its creation, he and now his newfound child—along with her amazing extended family of relatives and friends—have made him part of something larger and stronger than himself.

The earrings, yes, he decides. He'll return for them in the morning. He moves along the display window, looking for a suitable gift for his son-in-law—a kind, gentle man, but what the tribes used to call a warrior when circumstances warranted it. Come to think of it, his daughter is a warrior too.

A watch—yes! His son-in-law's current one looks shabby

and out-of-date. What if it fails him? Much of the man's professional life depends on split-second timing. A good, well-styled watch, but not one of those foolish ones that provide extraneous useless data. His son-in-law has at his disposal far more sophisticated and reliable devices than those.

Of course, his Christmas shopping is far from completed. There are two cats in the household, and cats always enjoy treats. There is a housekeeper—a handsome woman of an indeterminate age—who divides her time between his daughter's home and that of her best friend. And others of the couple's friends who have welcomed him and made him feel a part of their circle. Not to mention those on the reserve who urged him to make this extended trip.

So much shopping. And wrapping. And mailing. But what else has he to do with the fortune he's amassed over the years?

So much pleasure in finally having a reason to spend some of it.

Noises on the formerly silent, empty street interrupt his thoughts. Hard heels slapping on the pavement in a manner that reminds him of old Nazi war movies he's seen on TV. They are coming from the west, the direction in which his daughter's house lies. Coming close to him.

He turns away from the display window, peers into the misty night, but he can make out only dark shapes.

A low, almost imperceptible growl reaches his ears. That of a human, not an animal. His flesh ripples. He has heard such growls before, on the rez long ago when opposing factions allowed their passions to escalate to rage. Instinctively he whirls and tries to run, but one of the shapes rushes forward and a heavy hand falls upon his right shoulder, staying him. And then the others descend upon him, grabbing, pulling, shoving.

"Dirty old Indian," a rough voice says close to his ear. "You don't belong in this neighborhood."

"I have every right to be here—"

"Like hell you do." Another hand grabs his left arm, shakes it painfully.

"Probably planning to rob the jewelry store," another voice says. "That's what you bastards do when you come to our city, isn't it, Geronimo? Break into places, steal like the savages you are."

And then the blows begin to fall—on his head, shoulders, back. Hard shoes kick his legs, a fist slams into his abdomen and doubles him over. He tries to fight back, flailing with his arms and legs, but there are too many of them. The blows drive him to his knees, then topple him forward onto his side, his head striking the pavement.

The last thing he sees is a silver watch on the wrist of the first man to strike him.

The last thing he hears are the words, "You're lucky we don't kill you, Geronimo. The only good Indian is a dead Indian."

4:08 a.m.

Hy and I are used to receiving urgent phone calls in the middle of the night, most of them requiring immediate action. But the doorbell ringing at this hour? That was both unusual and alarming. Few people know our home address.

Hy was immediately at the ready, reaching for the .45 he keeps in his nightstand. I put a cautioning hand on his shoulder and said, "It's probably Elwood. I thought I heard him go out on one of his late-night rambles a while ago. He might've forgotten his key."

"Let's hope that's all it is."

We caught up our matching terry cloth robes, threw them on. As we started down the stairway, Hy said, "I love your dad, McCone, but why don't we just pin the key to his jacket?"

"He'd probably forget it was there. Nobody on Moose Lane in St. Ignatius locks his or her house."

I'd left the porch light of our Spanish-style house on, knowing Elwood might go out rambling, and I could see a pair of shapes through the glass panes beside the door. The back of my neck prickled. Those were cop shapes; something was very wrong. I disabled the security system and threw the door open. The officer who regularly patrolled this area, Winifred Sighesio, and her sometimes partner Jeff Barcy stood there, their faces tense. In an uncharacteristic gesture, Sighesio put her hand on my arm.

"Sorry to bother you this late, Ms. McCone, but it's necessary," she said. "May we come in?"

"Of course." I motioned them toward the living room.

Elwood. It has to be something to do with Elwood.

We all remained standing while Sighesio said, "An old man was found not far from here an hour and a half ago, badly beaten, unconscious, with a possible concussion and other injuries. Shabbily dressed, looked to be Native American. One of the EMTs found your card"—she nodded to me—"in his pocket. Your home, office, and cell numbers and this address were written on the back."

"Elwood!" His name burst out between the fingers I'd pressed to my lips. Hy had slipped the .45 into the pocket of his robe; he put both arms around me and pulled me back against his chest.

"A pro bono client, maybe?" Barcy said. "We can't figure any other reason you'd have passed out one of your cards to a homeless guy—"

"He's my father, goddamn it!"

"Your father?" Sighesio said in shocked tones. "We had no idea, Ms. McCone. The way he was dressed, we took him for a derelict…"

I blinked back tears. Through them I could see Barcy's eyes sizing up our large living room with its buttery leather furnishings, native-stone fireplace, and big flat-screen TV. How, his expression asked, could a raggedy old Indian fit into such a place?

"Where is he now?" I demanded.

"SF General's trauma unit."

"How is he? What exactly are his injuries?"

"From what the EMTs could tell me, he has a broken arm, a broken femur, cracked ribs, numerous lacerations, and possibly a concussion and internal injuries. He hadn't regained consciousness when they took him away in the ambulance."

My God!

Hy asked her how Elwood had been found. She told us an anonymous caller had spotted him lying in the doorway of a jewelry store on Chestnut and called 911.

I asked shakily, "Was my father robbed?"

"Apparently not. His wallet contained quite a bit of cash and one credit card, Visa, issued in 2012."

That was typical Elwood—one credit card, and he would pay the full balance every month.

"Any evidence on the scene?"

"Blood smears indicating he was attacked and beaten where he was found. Nothing to point to the perps."

"What about witnesses?"

"As you know, the business section of Chestnut is pretty densely populated with shops, restaurants, and residential quarters above them. But there's very little activity at this time of night. We're going to canvass the area, but"—she threw out her arms helplessly—"we're so short handed right now…"

"D'you know who'll be investigating the case?"

"Not yet."

"Well, whoever it is will have help from me."

"Now just wait a minute," Barcy blurted. "Department regulations specifically forbid—"

Sighesio silenced him with a look and a gesture. "Go wait outside, Jeff."

"But—"

"Just *go!*"

He went because she was the senior officer, but not before shooting her a resentful look.

"He needs sensitivity training," she apologized. "He's young, but if he doesn't grow up fast, he won't be with the PD much longer. You folks want a ride to SFG?"

"No," I said, "we'll drive ourselves."

5:37 a.m.

I was no stranger to the SF General campus, but the new Zuckerberg Trauma Center dwarfed the older buildings at the foot of Potrero Hill. The public had approved an $800,000-and-some-dollar bond measure a few years ago, but that amount covered only construction costs. Then Mark Zuckerberg, creator of Facebook, and his wife, Dr. Priscilla Chan, stepped in, donating $75 million to equip and furnish the facility.

Fewer years ago than I care to remember, I'd been a patient at the old trauma center, first in a coma and then in a bullet-generated locked-in state where I was fully aware but unable to speak, move, or communicate in any way. Fortunately for me, its excellent staff—and later the staff at the rehab center the hospital referred me to—brought me back to the woman I'd once been, and I feel an intense loyalty to both the hospital and the center. Hy and I have directed a number of our philanthropic efforts their way—but of course in amounts nowhere near those of megarich folks like Zuckerberg and Chan.

Hy let me off at the door of the trauma center and went off to find a place to park. I joined the line for emergency room visitors, but one of the admitting personnel motioned me over—a male nurse who'd befriended and visited me frequently when I was in my locked-in state. He took charge, cutting through the standard waiting time of nearly an hour, and soon Hy and I were speaking with Dr. David Stiles, the neurosurgeon assigned to Elwood's case.

As Sighesio had indicated, Elwood's condition was very

serious. He was in the intensive care unit and not allowed visitors at present. He still hadn't regained consciousness.

"He's strong for a man his age," Stiles said. "Do you have any idea of when he was born, Ms. McCone?"

"I don't know exactly, just that he's in his eighties, but I can get the information on…from other relatives tomorrow." I'd almost said "on the moccasin telegraph," which would require too much explanation to this straightforward man of science.

"Your father's bone density appears to be good. Breaks in the femur, the left arm, and the clavicle have been set. The two cracked ribs"—he shrugged—"all we could do was tape them."

He paused.

Oh God, here it comes!

"The most serious potential problem is traumatic brain injury. Do you know what that is?"

"I ought to. I was a patient here when I had locked-in syndrome."

"Ah—I thought your name was familiar. You're something of a legend around here. Let's hope your father is built of the same strong stuff you are." He paused, then went on, "Here's what else we're doing: CT scans, which will reveal if he has suffered a concussion and/or a subdural hematoma; bone density and various standard tests. If a blood clot has formed, or there are indications one may form, surgery will be necessary."

"Is he likely to have permanent brain damage?"

"At this point, we can't hazard a guess. The brain is tricky, and it varies its tricks from day to day. Every case is different. Your father may have suffered brain damage of varying severity, or he could wake up one morning and be perfectly fine. Only time will tell."

Since we couldn't see Elwood yet and wouldn't be able to for some time, Stiles suggested Hy and I return home. We would be notified immediately if there was any change in Elwood's condition. I wanted to stay anyway, but Hy talked me out of it.

"There's nothing for you to do at the hospital," he said, "and plenty at home."

He was right about that. It was now morning across the entire continent, and I had to face the unpleasant task of notifying our family members.

7:01 a.m.

Saskia Blackhawk, my birth mother—more about that later—in Boise, Idaho, had become close to Elwood in recent years, so to begin with I phoned her. She expressed shock, then full lawyer-mode anger and indignation. "I'll be at SFO on the first available flight and come directly to the hospital," she told me.

Saskia is an attorney dealing in Indian rights who has argued before federal courts and the Supreme Court, winning every case. When Elwood's attackers were found, her rage and legal expertise would make them pay the maximum penalty.

I asked her if she knew my father's exact birth date. She did: April 13, 1935. "Before I let you go," she said then, "please don't call your other mother. It's best I break the news to her myself."

"Why? Is Ma—"

"Just please let me do it. I'll explain when I see you."

Next I called Jane Nomee, a weaver of great skill and the reigning gossip queen of the moccasin telegraph. Jane, a tall, strong woman in her sixties, lived in St. Ignatius, the nearest town to Elwood's home.

The moccasin telegraph is a loosely linked group devoted to circulating information about all things Indian throughout the nation. Once, they claim, it operated on smoke signals—and maybe it did—but these days the Internet and smartphones transmit the necessary information. When anything noteworthy occurred, Jane would be on the phone or e-mail to those who would spread the word far and wide. When I'd first visited the reserve I'd found her intimidating. Now that I knew her better she was just Jane the Reporter.

I asked her to spread the word about the attack on Elwood, but to caution everyone to keep it strictly among themselves. Jane, who is a devotee of TV crime shows, agreed to get moving on Elwood's mishap. Soon, I was sure, the MT wires would be humming.

My most difficult call was to Will Camphouse in Tucson. He wasn't a relative of mine in the white-world sense, but—as he often claimed—he was my symbolic cousin. Whatever, he was the closest friend I had in the Indian part of my family.

Will said, "I already know what happened. Robin just called me."

Robin Blackhawk, my half sister who was in law school at Berkeley. Of course she knew; Saskia had probably phoned her to ask for a ride from SFO to SF General.

Will expressed the same anger and indignation that Saskia had, then asked, "You want me to come up there?"

"Not necessary—not yet."

"Well, don't hesitate to ask; I've just wrapped up a big campaign and have some time off coming." He was creative director at a large Tucson ad agency.

I closed my eyes, picturing hordes of the descendants of Chief Tendoy—leader of the Lemhi Shoshone from 1863 until his death in 1907—eventually convening at the hospital and in the Marina district, lobbying for Indian rights. The Shoshone are normally a gentle people, skilled in coping with adversity and hostility, but they've been pushed around enough by white society and the US government to go into explosive mode when circumstances warrant it.

The rest of my calls were not so difficult: My adoptive brother John, who lived in a downtown high-rise here in the city, was fond of Elwood and my Indian family and said he'd be on call for anything they needed. My nephew Mick Savage, chief researcher at the agency, had learned of the attack on the morning news and put out a staff bulletin. Then calls began pouring in from friends whom they'd contacted. I'd had no idea how many people cared about me and mine.

9:08 a.m.

Shortly after I finished speaking with the last well-wisher, a Sergeant Priscilla Anders from the SFPD assault division called and asked if she could come over and interview us about the attack. I agreed, did a quick spiff-up, and greeted her at the door.

Anders was an attractive woman of about sixty, wearing a conservative gray pantsuit to match her conservatively cut gray hair; a delicate silver necklace and matching bracelet were her only adornments. She showed me her identification and then followed me to the living room, where she accepted coffee from the pot Hy had just brewed and got right down to business.

"Your father normally resides where?" she asked me, snapping open a spiral-bound notebook.

"In St. Ignatius, Montana, on the Flathead Reservation."

"He is here visiting for the holidays?"

"Yes. He arrived two days ago and intends to stay through the New Year."

"I understand Mr. Farmer is in his eighties."

"Eighty-two." I told her his birth date.

"What does Mr. Farmer do in Montana? I assume he's retired?"

"No, he isn't. He's a nationally known painter and also tutors in various schools in the vicinity of the reservation."

Anders looked at her notes. I had the feeling she already knew most of the information I'd provided, but was checking for accuracy's sake.

I asked, "Have you turned up anything on the perps yet?"

"No," she replied with a frown. "Do you know if your father has any enemies?"

"In San Francisco? He's only been here two days."

"Someone who may have followed him from Montana?"

"That's extremely doubtful. He's a beloved figure throughout the state."

"Could the attack have been directed at you or Mr.

Ripinsky?" She nodded at Hy, who was sitting quietly in a chair near the fireplace. "Perhaps someone doing harm to your father-in-law as a way of harming you? Given the nature of your professions—private investigator and security services—you must have made a number of enemies."

Hy said, "Well, yes. But I doubt our relationship to Elwood is widely known."

"Are you sure of that?"

I said, "My father is a very private man. And my husband and I are as well, at least in our personal lives."

"Yet professionally you seem to have garnered more than your fair share of publicity, both local and national."

Hy moved restively—a caution not to give in to the emotional storm that he knew was building within me. To Anders he said, "My wife and I don't seek out attention, Sergeant. Our aim, as simple as it may seem to others, is to effect positive solutions for our clients."

"And I suppose these clients are always on the right side of the law?"

"Over the years, one or two who weren't have slipped through our background checks. But we pride ourselves on being thorough, and in the unlikely event we find someone has misrepresented himself or herself to us, we have a clause in our contract that releases us from their employ. And"— he smiled wryly—"that allows us to keep all fees that have already been paid to us. That's the point where the undesirables put down their pens and walk out."

"Excuse me," I said, "but what does all this have to do with the attack on my father? What is the SFPD doing in his case?"

Anders glanced at me, then looked away. "All we can. Mr. Ripinsky, have you represented some of these 'undesirables'?"

"Yes, we have. A few. Our relationships with them ended badly for all concerned."

Especially in our last major case that prompted the state and congressional hearings we'd been involved in for much of the past year. The hearings had concerned various individuals and corporations that, contrary to the public record, had committed crimes against the US during the violent times in Southeast Asia following the Vietnam War. When he fled the area, Hy had taken evidence from the charter service he'd worked for and turned it over to the CIA, but for years nothing had happened. When we decided to go public with the information, a number of highly placed and powerful people had fallen from grace; others had been convicted and were serving long sentences. Only two had escaped prosecution.

"And who are they specifically?" Anders asked.

"I can't recall all their names offhand, I'm afraid," Hy said. "And I don't see any of them doing what was done to Elwood as a form of payback."

"Ms. McCone?"

My back was up; Anders was following a standard routine of ignoring the female witness while catering to the male. All I said was, "Neither do I."

"You think the assault was random, then?"

"Not necessarily, but all the surface evidence points that way."

"A random attack in an affluent neighborhood upon an individual who didn't look as if he belonged there."

"An especially vicious attack," I said. "Very possibly by someone motivated by racial hatred."

Anders nodded as if I were a schoolkid who had given the right answer to a tricky question. "That would be my best guess as well, though it's too early to rule out other possibilities."

She stood up briskly, snapping her notebook shut. "I'll leave you now, but I'll want to talk with you tomorrow."

"You'll let us know right away if you come up with anything?"

"Naturally."

I shut the door behind her and said to Hy, "Kind of a cold woman, huh?"

"Yeah."

"Why, d'you think?"

"Could be many things."

"Not racial prejudice. I can sniff that out instantly. Not because she resents our financial status; her clothing and jewelry tell me she uses what she earns well."

"Could be that she doesn't like dealing with a firm like M&R."

M&R: McCone & Ripinsky. A few years ago we'd merged my investigative agency and his international executive protection firm into one entity. So far the merger had been successful, despite a number of snags along the way.

Hy went on, "We've snatched the solutions to prized investigations out of the SFPD's hands a few times."

Alex the cat entered the room, his tail switching, and sniffed the place where the inspector had been sitting.

I said, "She hates cats?"

We both burst into tension-easing laughter, and then the

landline rang. I picked up. A familiar voice, usually maternal but distinctively not so at the moment, said, "What the hell are you doing at home? Get your asses over here!"

"Ma?" The name came out weakly.

"Your father is lying here in the ICU, and what are you doing?"

"We've been talking with the police."

"Are you done with them?"

"Yes, just now."

"Then get your asses *over here*!" She hung up.

I met Hy's eyes. His were faintly amused. He'd heard every one of her shouted words.

"Okay," I said. "Okay, let's go."

11:10 a.m.

As we drove to the hospital, my thoughts were on my family. Ma has shrunk with age, and her formerly red hair has gone gray, but she is still strong, energetic, and very involved in life—her own and sometimes, unfortunately, those of her children and grandchildren. But she's a good, loving person and we all know we can rely on her in a crisis. Apparently now she needed to rely on us.

Because it was prime visiting hours at SFG, it seemed as though it took us ages to find a parking space in the emergency unit lot. I'd girded myself for chaos inside, but the waiting area and halls were surprisingly quiet; the only sounds were the clicking of the computer keyboards at the intake desk and the rustle of the magazine pages that those waiting for news of relatives and friends idly flipped through. I didn't recognize either of the two nurses, but that wasn't surprising; a long time had passed since I was rushed to the trauma unit, and at the time I'd been unconscious with a bullet lodged in my brain.

I went up to the desk and asked about Elwood. His condition hadn't changed, and he still wasn't allowed visitors. The nurse summoned an aide, who guided us to a smaller room where Ma waited.

Fortunately she didn't chastise us for our tardiness. In fact, she drew us close and sniffled into my coat. Hy and I looked at each other over her head: two redwoods towering above a little quaking aspen.

I took a tissue from a pack in my pocket and unfolded it for her. After a moment she released us, stepped back, and gave the Kleenex two of what she called her "goose honks."

She said, "You talked to the police. What're they doing?"

"Investigating."

"Do they have any leads yet?"

"Not yet."

"Well, they'd better find the sons of bitches who did this! That's somebody I care about lying in there."

Katie McCone had come a long way since she used to scold us kids about our "salty" language, I thought as she clutched me and burst into tears again.

3:31 p.m.

The necessary tests were still going on. That's all the doctors and nurses could tell us, until just before Saskia and Robin arrived. Then Dr. Stiles came in with word that the CT scan had revealed what I'd been dreading: both a concussion and a subdural hematoma. Elwood was being prepped for brain surgery.

"The prognosis is fair," he told us. "For a man in his eighties, he's incredibly fit. The surgery will take several hours; the best thing you people can do for yourselves is to go home. You'll be informed as soon as we have the results of the surgery."

It was the second time the doctor had told us to go home. Was this what it was going to be like? To-ing and fro-ing and hanging on tenterhooks for hours, even days, while we waited for news?

The elevator beeped and Saskia stepped through its doors. She is a tall woman, maybe five foot ten, with thick silver-black hair that she customarily gathers into braids that she coils about her head. We strongly resemble one another in our high cheekbones and the tilt of our noses.

Saskia had been very young when she became pregnant with me—the result of a one-night stand with Elwood shortly before he moved to New York to pursue his painting. My birth mother was poor and about to enter college on a scholarship; no way could she raise a child. She arranged—by way of a mutual relative—to have me adopted by Andrew and Katie McCone, who'd told me my looks were a "throwback" to my Indian grandmother. When I found out about their lies and half truths I'd been enraged, but that was years ago, and by now I'd become close to both my families, as thoroughly dysfunctional as both were.

Ma was very pale; Saskia hugged her and told her to go

downstairs and wait for my sister Patsy to arrive after having gotten one of her employees to close out her Napa Valley restaurant for the evening. As soon as the elevator doors closed behind Ma, I asked Saskia, "What was it you wanted to explain to me?"

"You know your mother and I have become close."

"Yes."

"She has become emotionally fragile recently."

"How so?"

"Too much loss in her life—your father, her second husband, one of your brothers. She cries easily. Talks of death a lot."

"How long has this been going on?"

"A few months. You haven't noticed it?"

"No, we haven't been in touch as much as usual."

I thought about Ma's present circumstances. A year ago she'd moved from San Diego to the Monterey Peninsula and seemed happy there, but maybe I hadn't been listening carefully. She'd made friends, thrown herself into painting her watercolors, but now that I thought about it, there had been a hollow note in her voice during our frequent phone calls. And her reaction to Elwood's condition had been uncharacteristically emotional...

Before I could ask Saskia anything more, Ma returned with Patsy. Hy and I went downstairs to the business office to complete the necessary paperwork to arrange for Elwood's care.

When we got back upstairs, Patsy was looking ragged.

She whispered, "No way I can take any more crying."

"Me either."

Hy said, "Then we're out of here. Your mother won't notice—the doctor's making his rounds and soon she'll have a new audience." He swept his arm toward the door. "After you two, please."

4:46 p.m.

Instead of going home, we drove to the M&R building. It was a beautifully restored Vermont granite structure—circa 1932—on New Montgomery Street in the city's thriving financial district. We leased the ground floor to a number of upscale clothing shops, as well as the famous Angie's Deli, where we whiled away many a lunch hour in the outdoor dining section. The top three stories of the building were ours.

On floor two our case and financial files were encoded and stored; the personnel department operated out of there too. Clerks tabulated operatives' hours and expenses. Building services and maintenance people checked in for their daily schedules. Floor three consisted of hospitality suites: at-risk clients could reside there confident of their safety; operatives from our offices in other cities were welcomed; large functions such as parties and dinners were hosted.

But the heart and soul of the M&R building was the fourth floor and the roof garden. The offices of the core employees—including Hy and me—were elegant. Deep, gray carpets a couple of shades darker than the walls. Beautiful but functional rosewood furnishings. Colorful framed posters depicting special events throughout the city over the years. And the roof garden was a splendid place to entertain clients or just chill out.

We left the car in the underground garage, then walked

to a favorite restaurant near the waterfront. Its interior was pseudo–old San Francisco—heavy gilt-framed mirrors, ornately carved wooden bar, and cozy red-plush booths—but lacking the colorful characters and elaborate free-lunch buffets that had typified the saloons of the city in bygone days. Back in the Gay Nineties the men entering the saloons could feast on a banquet of everything from meats and seafood to the ever-popular terrapin—after purchasing a beer for only ten cents. The bankers and attorneys and businessmen who worked downtown would join the parade that was known as the Cocktail Route by midafternoon and carouse through the evenings, often into the mornings. Marriages would die, children would be left fatherless, but the march continued.

No wild goings-on here, however, in this new century. During the late afternoon only a pair of well-dressed businessmen played liar's dice at the bar, while a single similarly stylish woman read a magazine and sipped a glass of wine in one of the booths.

"When we come here, do you ever get the idea," Hy said, "that we've stepped back into history?"

"With all this crap I carry around?" I indicated my bag, which contained an iPad, an ultra-high-resolution camera, a flashlight, and a packet of surgical gloves and another of plastic evidence bags. To say nothing of my .38 Special—the gun I've tried to replace with one with more firepower, more accuracy, and a lighter frame, but to which I keep coming back. "Of course we live in a new world."

Patsy said, "But is it a *brave* new world?"

I considered. "Not hardly, if we need all this stuff to protect and connect ourselves."

The bartender came over. "You three look like you could use a drink."

"Yep," Hy said. "Bourbon straight up for me."

I said, "Chardonnay, please."

Patsy, who spends the majority of her life around food and drink, made a face and said, "Black coffee, with orange juice on the side."

"You sure she's with you?" the barman asked.

"She's an abstainer," I said.

He shrugged. "There's an oddball in every crowd."

The look Patsy shot at his departing back would have melted a steel girder. "If any one of my servers ever spoke that way about a customer, he'd've been out the door before he could set down his tray."

"Restaurant protocol isn't our main concern at the moment," I said.

Our drinks arrived, and I took a healthy swig of mine. Patsy stared longingly at it and flagged down the waiter to ask for one.

I looked at her, and she shrugged and said, "I decided I need an antidote too."

"For what?"

"All the wailing Ma was doing, like she was about to have a breakdown."

"Saskia says she's been 'emotionally fragile' for a few months. What do you suppose that's all about? Her reaction seemed like she was upset by more than the attack on Elwood."

"In a way she was. You know about their purported 'engagement'?"

"What!" Hy and I said together.

"Oh, so you don't know." Patsy shook her head. "It's bizarre. Truly bizarre. She's somehow gotten the idea into her head that they're having a romance and will be getting married."

This was way more news than I could take in. I stared at Patsy and finally asked, "When did you find out about it?"

"While you guys were downstairs. I didn't know she was seeing him at all until then. And…well, they're kind of old."

I said, "They're not 'kind of' old—they're *old.*"

"So what do they want with each other?"

"The same thing we all do. Wouldn't you want somebody to warm your tootsies when you're in your eighties?"

Patsy looked thoughtful, then grinned. "Why do you think I've been entertaining tootsie warmers my whole adult life? None of them have measured up, and I sure hope one does before I'm Ma's age. But what I mean by bizarre is the way the news came out of nowhere. Saskia didn't believe it, and I was totally sandbagged. Do *you* believe it?"

"No," I said, and glanced at Hy. He shook his head.

"It's probably just another one of her fantasies," Patsy said.

That gave me another pause. "She has fantasies?"

"Well, sure. You haven't noticed?"

"No."

"She's been having them since I was a little girl. I guess because I'm the youngest and was the last one left in the nest, she acted out the fantasies more in front of me. When Pa had gone away on deployment, she claimed he was really doing missions for the CIA. When he was away for long hours, there had to be another woman. When he went around singing those dirty songs—which I rather liked—they were a code for something." She shut her eyes, shook her head.

"I didn't know anything about any of this!"

"She kept herself in control when you were home. You were always her favorite."

I put my hand on Patsy's arm. "No, I wasn't. I couldn't do a damn thing right. She rode me like crazy."

"That's what you do with favorites; I pick on Jessamyn until the kid thinks I'm the devil incarnate."

I pictured my mother's life; she had a lovely three-bedroom house with a view of the ocean in Pacific Grove. On the other hand, Elwood lived in a log cabin on the Flathead rez that he'd built himself upon his return from New York City many years ago. It was ringed by lodgepole pines, snug and cozy, but I couldn't imagine Ma stoking the woodstove in the morning or ascending the ladder to the sleeping loft at night, any more than I could imagine Elwood being comfortable in Pacific Grove. He wouldn't even consider such arrangements. No way.

I said, "It's got to be a figment of her imagination. Besides, Elwood's been staying at our house; he would've mentioned it to one or the other of us if it were true."

Hy said, "And he certainly hasn't. In fact, he'd been talking to me about the three of us taking one of those small-ship cruises to Alaska."

"You and him and Ma?" I asked.

"No, dummy—you and me and him." He paused, frowning. "You don't suppose she's seriously disturbed, do you?"

"As in needing hospital care? I hope not."

Patsy didn't look so sanguine, but then she said, "She usually snaps back from these lapses pretty quick. As long as Elwood doesn't...well, you know."

As long as Elwood doesn't die, she meant.

Neither Hy nor I said anything.

Patsy bit her lip. "Well," she said then, "let's not get ahead of ourselves. I'm going back to the hospital. I'll fetch Ma and Saskia and take them to John's condo. It's only a short distance away, and I've already okayed it with him."

I said, "Thank you, Pats, but for safety's sake, I think it's better if they stay in one of the M&R hospitality suites." I wrote down the information she'd need to get them situated. "And since Ma's wearing on you, why don't you stay in our guest room?"

"Thanks. I appreciate it."

I looked at my watch. "I'd better go—I've got a staff meeting in ten minutes."

5:45 p.m.

When I got to the agency, my staff members were already settled at the big round table in the conference room. The table was completely at variance with the rest of the furnishings in our suite: badly banged up, with evidence of spilled meals and drinks, fists pounded in rage at their owners' losses at poker games or Monopoly, maybe even some tearstains in the mix. For years it had stood in the kitchen at All Souls Legal Cooperative, the poverty law firm where I'd then been employed. When the co-op shut down, none of us could bear to part with it and its memories, so it had followed whichever of us had room for it. I liked to think of this place as its final home.

Before I could enter the conference room, Derek Frye—a slender, handsome man of Japanese descent with a colorful tattoo of snakes around his neck—pulled me aside. "Mick suggested I look up Indian advocacy groups on the chance that the attack on your father wasn't random but a targeting of Native Americans. Most of the big groups—like the California Indian Legal Services—are located in Sacramento or the areas with large populations of Natives, like Escondido, Bishop, and Eureka. I called Sacto and they steered me to one here in the city—a co-op of lawyers and social workers called Change and Growth. They'll be able to tell you about the status of Indians in the Bay Area. And—although the CILS woman didn't overtly state it, she implied that they may have information on local crime against Natives."

"How do I get hold of them?"

"You have an appointment tomorrow afternoon with Sylvia Blueflute, their San Francisco representative." He handed me a sheet with details.

The staff meeting began on time, in spite of the unusually late hour. "According to the police report," I began, "the attack on my father occurred sometime between midnight, when a witness saw him crossing Bay Street near Francisco, and two twelve a.m. He was lying in front of a jewelry store on Chestnut Street when a passing motorist spotted him and called the police." I was trying to keep my voice level, but the image of Elwood bloodied and broken and tossed away like a heap of old clothing was nearly too much for me. I paused, closing my eyes. Then I composed myself and went on, "He was badly beaten and uncommunicative. Was taken to SFG emergency, where the doctors are performing surgery to relieve pressure on his brain. The SFPD assault unit has given us permission to assist them. As you know, they're short handed, and we've done them a few favors in the past. Sergeant Priscilla Anders, the officer in charge of the investigation, and her team are presently canvassing residents in the area for witnesses, but not a lot of people were awake or out and about at the time the assault happened. But there's still the possibility that somebody heard something or might've glanced out the window at the right time."

"So we divide the area up into sectors and canvass it too?" Julia Rafael, a tall, good-looking Latina, asked.

"Right. Derek has already divided it and is considering which available operatives should be assigned to a sector. We may have to co-opt people from another agency. Please speak to him about it. Keep in mind that in neighborhoods like the Marina, people are not exactly forthcoming, in fact they can be downright testy about answering questions."

Derek said, "The research department's also interfacing with the residents in the area, as well as checking on other attacks that might be racially motivated. We're contacting people who have been tracking hate crimes, as well as people who live in the area where the crimes have occurred."

I asked, "Any luck so far?"

"No, but we'll keep at it."

Julia raised her hand. "The police—have they given us permission to investigate however we choose?"

"Yes."

"And they'll report to us anything the PD comes up with?"

"Right. But don't count on them coming up with much. They're into their usual chaotic state over there."

"I thought this new chief they brought in was supposed to fix that."

"He will. He's a good cop. But you can't clean up a mess like he's faced with overnight."

Roberta Cruz, the newest addition to our team, asked, "What about this 'passing motorist' who called it in? Did he identify himself?"

"No."

"Can anybody get a fix on who he is?"

"Just the number that came up on the screen at the 911 switchboard. It was a mobile phone, which makes it trickier, but not impossible, to trace to the owner. I'm pretty sure the cops are working on it. But I'll check with Anders to make sure."

"Give the number to me," Derek said. "I can do it easier than the cops can."

I wrote it down and passed the paper to him.

Mick, who had rushed in late, said, "I know you're approaching this as a random crime, but did it occur to anyone that it could be tied to an old case? Like this past year's congressional hearings?"

I thought. "Most of the people involved are in federal prison, but a couple got off scot-free. I'll check my files, see if I can locate them, and follow up."

Mick said, "What about other cases?"

"I'll deal with them too."

Mick looked annoyed.

"Any other questions?" I asked. "No? Then let's get out there and find the assholes who did this."

7:10 p.m.

I'd just pulled into my driveway when Dr. Stiles called to tell me Elwood had survived the surgery and the blood clot on his brain had been relieved. Greatly relieved myself, I sucked in a deep breath of the cool evening air. The prognosis for Elwood's full recovery was still dependent on his strength and recuperative powers, Stiles said, but there was cause for cautious optimism.

"We can all only hope to be as constitutionally strong at his age," he added.

When I relayed the news to Hy, he said, "Elwood's a tough old bird. He'll be all right."

"God, I hope so."

"He will be. I'm sure of it."

Yes. So was I.

I asked, "Those congressional hearings we testified at—do you recall the names of the two people who went free?"

"Yeah—Melanie Jacobs and Arthur Wight. I think they both lived in the Bay Area. Why? Do you think they're connected with this current trouble?"

"Seems a long shot, but I'm going to look into it."

While I was hanging up my jacket, he said, "This is a bad time to look for, much less try to talk with, anyone. Have you even thought about Christmas? It's only six days away, and our Christmas Eve dinner with Rae and Ricky only five days."

"I haven't, what with all that's been going on. You?"

"Nope. Maybe we should. It might help take our minds off the grim stuff for a while."

"Just what I was thinking. Tell you what: I'll build a fire while you uncork a bottle of that good Zin from the Alexander Valley. And we'll call that Italian restaurant on Twenty-Fourth Street that delivers. Then we'll make a plan."

7:53 p.m.

The Christmas list we made out struck me as kind of pathetic.

Elwood: No way of knowing what he needed or wanted. A return to good health, we couldn't give him.

Ma: She'd always been big on Christmas, but she wouldn't be this year. We'd have her over for dinner and give her small gifts. Saskia and Robin would join us. As I thought of my second family, I said, "I forgot to send Darcy his candy." One of the few constants in my crazy half brother's life is a love of peanut brittle.

"There's still time if it goes FedEx." Hy noted it on a legal pad he held.

"Rae and Ricky?"

"An ornament for their tree. You remember how they loved the handblown glass cat? And maybe some stuff from L.L.Bean or Lands' End."

"Right. Charlene and Vic?"

"They don't need anything. A call to them in London—where they should be arriving about now—from all of us should suffice."

"Ricky and Charlene's kids?"

"Gift cards, except for Mick."

"And Mick?"

"A brand-new Thirty-Eight Special to replace that old forty-five of yours that he keeps in the safe at the office."

"Good idea. I never should've given him the forty-five anyway. It's a piece of shit. What about John?"

"A telescope so he can view the city from his new condo."

"Patsy and family? I know. Some obscure kitchen gizmo that will baffle the hell out of them."

"What about the folks at the agency?"

"I've already distributed the bonuses."

"Ted and Neal?" My office manager and his longtime partner.

"They wanted one of these things." I pointed at a beautiful hand-carved wooden stand that sat on the end table beside me. "They hold up books or anything else while you're reading."

"Elegant. Can we get them on time?"

"I've had them since September."

We kept on going down the list until we reached the point of "Others—phone calls or the Christmas cards I bought last summer."

I sighed. "We're done."

"Not by a long shot," he told me. "Now we've got to buy and wrap all this stuff."

11:11 p.m.

We'd taken our list and gotten on Internet sites that promised next-day delivery and gift wrapping. Everything was in stock and ready to ship. All was well with the holiday world.

But not our world. Not unless Elwood fully recovered, and not until the bastards who assaulted him were behind bars.

WEDNESDAY, DECEMBER 20

8:25 a.m.

How could you have let me sleep so long?" I asked Hy
when he woke me with a gentle hand on my shoulder.

"Because you badly needed to." He sat down on the bed.
"I was being overprotective, and I'm sorry. But you've had
some pretty heavy things on your plate recently. So have I.
And I'm sure Patsy—who's currently sleeping in the guest
room—has too; the restaurant business is pretty brutal, especially at the holidays."

Patsy had begun her career as a restaurateur when she
bought a dilapidated resort on an island in the Sacramento
Delta, planning to turn it into a bed-and-breakfast. The
experiment had not been a success. But when she tried a
similar venture in Napa, Patsy's Place had taken off, and she
was now bargaining for a second in Sonoma.

9:29 a.m.

Before I left the house, I received a call from Jane Nomee
in Montana, wanting to give me some information she

37

hadn't recalled during our short conversation yesterday.

"I don't know if this is pertinent to what happened to Elwood or not," she said, "but I thought you ought to know. A few years ago, this white guy arrived in St. Ignatius. Claimed to be an artist and started asking around about Elwood. It turned out he really was an artist; he tried to sell his paintings to the only gallery in town, the Eagle's Nest, but—the then owner told me—they weren't very good, so she turned him away. Said something didn't seem quite right about him. And the people in town, they were protective of Elwood, so nobody pointed the man his way."

"Did he give anyone his name?"

"If he did, nobody remembers it."

"Can you describe him?"

"A normal, white-bread young guy. Flaming red hair, shades and boots and clothes like they show in the hunters' catalogs. I'm fairly accurate on this information. Last night I had a short conversation with Mingan—excuse me, I sometimes revert to the old ways—with Will, and he refreshed my memory."

"Mingan—what does that mean in English?"

"Gray Wolf. He was so fierce as a child. But about this artist…is it possible he's involved in the assault on Elwood for some reason?"

"Possible, but not likely. Anyhow, there's no way I can investigate him without knowing his name."

"I'm sorry I can't provide you with one. I was postmistress at the time—before the government took the office away—and no letters or packages came for him. He stayed for a week at the Wigwam motel, on the northern side of town. It's out of business now."

I'd stayed at the Wigwam on an early visit to St. Ignatius—twelve shabby units where everything was screwed in place to walls or floor, presumably so guests wouldn't steal it. I'd wondered why anyone would want to.

"Do you have any idea what happened to the motel's registration records?"

"Up in smoke. The drunken owner incinerated himself, the motel, and all its contents three years ago."

"Do you have the owner's full name or any information about his next of kin?"

She hesitated. "I don't know anything about his family or where he came from. Anyway," she went on, "the artist was very interested in meeting Elwood. This was right after Elwood's wife Leila died in the car wreck, so we didn't want him bothering Elwood and wouldn't give him information about his whereabouts. You know what, though: you might call my daughter Emi. She bought the Eagle's Nest—and remembers the so-called artist trying to peddle his paintings to the previous owner. They were pretty bad, she says, all bloody battle scenes. But if he really *was* trying to peddle something, he would've given his name, right?"

"Right. Actually, I know Emi. The last time I was up there she was director of a youth-and-family services organization. Why the change?"

"Budget cuts. Nobody in Washington cares about Indian youth or families."

I couldn't deny that.

I copied down Emi's contact information, then began phoning her various numbers.

12:47 p.m.

Emi proved difficult to track down. Her cell went to voice mail, the landlines to machines. At the Eagle's Nest Gallery, the young woman who answered against a background of rap music said, "Whazzat? Hang on, got to turn the tube down."

I repeated my request to talk to Emi Nomee.

"Oh, the bitch." She let loose with a high-pitched giggle. "I mean the boss." More giggling.

Stoned. Stoned in the middle of the day and on the job.

"When is Ms. Nomee expected back?" I asked sharply.

"I dunno," she replied. "She went away."

"Went away where?"

"San Francisco."

"That's where I'm calling from."

"Yeah? Cool."

And she broke the connection without saying anything else.

I gave a short moment of thought to what was currently called "the dumbing down of America." Then I decided it probably wasn't worth my time and set off for the M&R building.

2:15 p.m.

And there she was, pacing the hallway like a tigress about to pounce. Ma.

I hugged her and asked, "What are you doing here?" as I led her back to my office. "I thought you'd be at the hospital."

She made a huffing sound and plopped into one of the chairs. "I don't go where I'm not wanted."

"Who doesn't want you there?"

"That nurse—the one with the fat ass. And that attendant who's always so cheery."

I studied her. Her complexion was mottled and there were large pouches under her reddened eyes.

"Maybe they just think you need some rest and regular meals."

"I'll rest when I'm dead. And I don't see you taking me into your home and feeding me."

"Ma, I'm involved in finding out who attacked Elwood. You want that, don't you?"

Silence. She stared straight ahead at the wall.

"And you don't like my cooking," I added.

"Hy's is not bad."

"He's working on this too. As well as a number of other cases."

A tear appeared on her lashes and trickled down her left cheek.

Oh God, she's going into her fallback mode!

My mother cried only when nothing else worked.

And, as usual, it did work. "Look, Ma, why don't you go downstairs to the hospitality suite and rest? Then put on that great dress—the sapphire-blue one. Come back around six, and we'll have cocktails and go out someplace nice for dinner."

She brightened at once. "That sounds good. I'll see you then."

When Ma was gone, I collapsed onto my office couch feeling defeated once again. I'd relapsed into behavior that I despised.

It's hard to be Old Reliable.

By that I mean the one everybody—family, friends, and employees—depends on. The go-to girl they know will be able to fix things.

Need help with settling that overdue bill? Ask Shar.

The bank statement's fucked up? Shar's got a friend at your branch who will help you.

You didn't *what*?...Okay, Shar will take care of it.

Shar must know a good auto mechanic, can probably get you a discount too. Shar understands how to get discounts...She's good with power tools...She likes kids, even if she hasn't got any of her own...I'm sure she'd be glad to fly you to Reno two hours from now...She understands health insurance...Short of cash? Ask Shar.

It had been that way my whole life, from the moment I rescued a little neighbor boy's kitten that had gotten stuck in the tree outside my bedroom window. I enjoyed being able to help others.

But often I wondered, what about *me*?

Who would rescue *my* kitten? (If I had one.)

Pity party coming on. No good.

I had better things to do than feel sorry for myself.

5:00 p.m.

Ted Smalley, our office manager, came into my office to bring me up to date on recent happenings. Today he was dressed in a checked sport coat, a wide tie—one of the wildest pink, green, and orange in the universe—pegged pants, and lizard-skin loafers.

"Nice duds," I said.

"Oh, I don't know. The coat and tie are okay, but I'm not sure the pants and shoes are authentic."

Ted is a self-admitted clothing fanatic. He goes through phases: Edwardian, surfer bum, Victorian, grunge, Roaring Twenties, and Colonial—to name a few. He should have been a costumer for a major Hollywood studio.

"What's the fashion statement this week?" I asked.

"Can't you tell?"

"No."

"Late sixties to midseventies. *Mannix* style."

"What's a mannix?"

"Oh, Shar, I despair of you. *Mannix* was a major TV show, starring Mike Connors; he always wore Botany 500."

"What's Botany 500?"

"Did you spend your time back then in a cave?"

"Apparently I must have. Where can you buy Botany 500 clothes now?"

"Can't. They went bankrupt long ago."

If what he had on was any example of their work, I wasn't surprised.

"Where do you find this stuff? Amazon?"

He smiled. "Trade secret."

"What does Neal think of it?"

Neal was Ted's husband. It had always seemed to me an unlikely relationship: Neal was a rare-books dealer with clients all over the world; his appearance was correct almost to the point of being stodgy. Ted was…well, Ted. But it worked beautifully.

"Neal thinks it's one of my better fashion statements. Of course, he loved the *Mannix* show."

• • •

Emi Nomee had flown down here to be with Elwood and lend moral support to her mother's best friend, Saskia. She was a strongly built woman, her black hair haphazardly piled on top of her head. This told me that she was aware of how handsome she was, but didn't want to flaunt it.

She'd come up to my office immediately upon her arrival so we could talk before Ma arrived for the cocktail hour.

I related what her mother had told me about the artist who'd come to St. Ignatius looking for Elwood. "What do you remember about him?" I asked.

"Well, he was short, almost gnomelike, with flaming red hair and an aggressive manner. Everybody wondered about him because he holed up in his room at the Wigwam most of the time. It didn't puzzle me; there's really nothing to do in town, unless you're interested in drinking to excess. Besides, maybe he'd had a rough trip from wherever he lived— New England, I think—and needed to rest."

He *could* be one of the thugs who'd attacked my father. There was just no way to tell without more information.

"You can't remember his name?"

"No. Sorry."

"But you do remember his paintings."

"I wish I couldn't. They were horrible, violent."

"I understand they were all battle scenes."

"Cavalry versus Indians, Little Bighorn stuff."

"With the Indians getting the worst of it?"

"No. Almost all the victims were soldiers. Twisted limbs, lots of blood—you know, all distorted and weird."

"Like Bosch."

"Except this guy lacked Bosch's talent."

We both fell silent for a time. Then Emi said, "I understand you spoke with my daughter on the phone earlier."

"Oh, was that your daughter?"

"Yes. I phoned my gallery a while ago and she told me there'd been a call from 'some woman in San Francisco.' I assumed it was you. She didn't give you any trouble, did she?"

"Well…she was a little vague."

"Stoned, you mean. She was when I talked to her. She usually is, these days. Three therapists, and nothing took hold. I hope she wasn't rude to you. She sometimes is when she's high."

"No, she wasn't. I'm used to teenagers; my sisters have several of them, and they spend a lot of time with me."

"Then you should be nominated for sainthood. One Astral Plane is more than enough for this world."

"I'm sorry. Who?"

"That's what my daughter's calling herself—now."

"She didn't tell me her name. It's…different."

"It's awful. She changes it every month, and goes into a rage if you don't instantly recognize and use it."

Well, Astral Plane was marginally better than SlumBag or Fuggit.

They were the current claimants to the top of the pop music charts.

Emi said, "I swear it's the ten thousand and fifty-fifth reason I've counted for not having children. But you shouldn't have to listen to my gripes about my poor parenting skills."

5:50 p.m.

After Emi left I went down the hall to Mick's office. My nephew was slumped in his desk chair, contemplating his tennis shoes, which were propped next to his keyboard.

"I have a lead for you." I told him about the artist who had traveled to St. Ignatius to see Elwood. "You think you can find out who he was?"

"These paintings—violent battle scenes—they weren't very good?"

"Not according to Emi, and she owns a gallery."

"So we wouldn't be able to find them in a museum."

"Not likely."

"Hmmm. I've got a friend at Berkeley. Her area of interest is what she calls the 'alternative arts.' The works can be good or bad, but more often they're bad. Or the subject matter is warped. For instance, the guy back in the seventies who only painted celebrities riding on sheep."

"You've got to be kidding."

"Nope. They became very popular, made him a lot of money. Now I suppose they're stashed in attics. I'll give her a call, see if she can shed some light on who this 'artist' is."

I thanked him and went to my office to await my cocktail party guests.

When they arrived, Saskia's and Robin's tired faces indicated they'd been keeping a long vigil at the hospital.

Robin also strongly resembles me, even though she and I had different fathers. Robin is the result of Saskia's happy marriage to a Boise attorney, Thomas Blackhawk, who put her through law school but had not lived long enough to see her career blossom. Darcy was also Thomas

Blackhawk's child, but some component had been left out of him.

No, components, plural: such as impulse control; logic; understanding the effects of one's actions. Add to those basic problems drug and alcohol addiction, pathological lying, a sometimes uncontrollable temper, paranoia—and, well, there you've got a dangerous mix.

Fortunately, for now at least, Darcy was residing in a clinic near Denver with tight security and a staff who seemed to know how to deal with him. But he had been in such places before. If he kept running away or getting kicked out of them, we'd eventually deplete the supply in several states.

Saskia said, "The no-visitors rule is still in force, but Dr. Stiles allowed us to look in on Elwood briefly. He used to be so tall and robust, but now he looks shrunken. And the lines on his face have deepened."

Robin—short, with her black hair caught up in a ponytail tied with a long red scarf—added, "All those monitors beeping and displaying lines and zigzags on their screens— they're downright creepy."

I flashed back to my own hospital bed, where I'd been tethered to tubes and IVs. I'd been unable to speak, move, or communicate in any way.

Robin saw the look on my face and said, "Oh, sorry, Shar. That must bring back bad memories."

"Yes, but I survived. So will Elwood."

"Maybe," Saskia said, "it would be better for you if you didn't visit him so often. Better emotionally, I mean."

"No. When I was locked in, Elwood came all the way from Montana to see me, at a time when we barely knew each other. He talked to me and kept me going. I need to do the same for him, even if he can't hear me."

Ma arrived, with Emi in tow.

"I'll make some drinks," I said, feeling a sudden need for one. This was going to be one hell of an evening. Having them converge on me made me feel like someone trapped in a revolving door that would spew her out wherever she was needed.

Yes, indeed, it's hard to be Old Reliable.

Saskia touched my shoulder and said, "Don't put yourself to all that trouble. We can have drinks at the restaurant. I'll call for one of those cars. It should be here shortly. We'll wait for it downstairs."

"You go ahead. I'll be along in a few minutes. I need to use the restroom."

I didn't need to, it was just an excuse. Instead I poured myself a glass of straight bourbon and guzzled it down.

9:57 p.m.

The dinner at Boulevard had been long and tedious, the conversation full of strained silences. After I'd made sure everyone was tucked into a WeDriveU car—the service the agency has an account with—I fetched my Mercedes from the M&R underground garage and drove to SFG to visit Elwood.

Luckily, there was no one on the floor desk, so I slipped into Elwood's room. He seemed to be resting quietly. I took the hand that wasn't in a cast and held it. His fingers, contrary to my expectation, were neither cold nor brittle.

I put my lips to his ear. "Father," I said. "It's Sharon."

Did I imagine a slight twitch?

"I know you can't tell me anything now, but I'm looking for the people who did this to you."

Motion around his dry lips. He seemed semiconscious now and aware of what I was saying. Then he became agitated, moving his head from side to side. I rang for the nurse.

She came at once. "No, he still hasn't regained consciousness," she said after examining him. "He must have been having a nightmare. Your presence isn't helping him. You do not have permission to be here."

"He's my father."

"And I'm his nurse."

God, I'd forgotten how bossy they could be!

I just stood there, looking at Elwood.

The nurse firmly grasped my elbow. "Ms. McCone, you have to go. You don't understand hospital routine and protocol."

I let her usher me out, but then I said, "I understand them all too well. Haven't you heard? I'm a legend here: the locked-in lady. There's very little about hospitals that I don't know."

THURSDAY, DECEMBER 21

8:32 a.m.

As I was about to leave home, Derek phoned with the name of the "anonymous caller" who had reported Elwood's beating to the SFPD, Don Taber, and the man's contact information. Taber lived and worked in San Mateo, on the Peninsula, which fit perfectly with my morning's plans.

"Am I still invited to Christmas dinner?" Derek asked.

"Of course! We're not letting anybody spoil that."

I didn't bother calling Mick; if he'd gotten anywhere on the search for the mysterious artist of ultraviolent paintings, he would have contacted me immediately. I grabbed my purse and set off to question the two individuals who had avoided imprisonment after last year's congressional hearings and who might hold enough of a grudge against me to attack a member of my family.

Hayes Valley, near the Civic Center and various performing arts venues, has, since 1989's Loma Prieta earthquake brought the oppressively looming Central Freeway crashing down, become an ultrachic place to live, eat, and shop. Galleries and eclectic restaurants—anything from French to

Asian to southern Brazilian—abound. Shops offer choice merchandise from far-flung corners of the earth. All of this, of course, adds up to expensive. The Well Knit Lady, owned by Melanie Jacobs, was no exception, although the goods displayed in its windows were more conservative than those in the other stores' windows: suits and dresses one might wear to a ladies' luncheon and a gown suitable for attending the opera or symphony.

I went inside and came face-to-face with Melanie, a short woman with frizzy black hair and a sharp nose. Her lipstick was bright red, her eyes overly made up, and her expression, when she saw me, outraged.

"You," she said. "How dare you come in here!"

"This is an interesting shop you have, Melanie." I looked around, then touched a blue-toned alpaca cape; its price tag read $8,500. "You've done well since the hearings."

"No thanks to you!"

She had been accused of bankrolling an arms dealer to ship weapons to Southeast Asia. Unfortunately, there hadn't been enough evidence in Hy's files to indict her.

I moved along to a selection of cashmere sweaters, for which the lowest price was $600. "These are lovely."

Some of her initial hostility had leaked out of Melanie Jacobs. She leaned her back against the sales counter, her arms crossed. "I've done better during the past year than ever. Sometimes negative publicity like having my name linked to those congressional hearings helps. If people come in out of curiosity or pity, I can usually sell them twice what I normally would."

"You still have hard feelings toward Hy and me?"

She shrugged. "Not really. I did what I did. So did you. It's all behind me now, and I'm smiling all the way to the bank."

I believed her.

One line of investigation closed.

9:41 a.m.

Someone once described Daly City to me as "San Francisco with an acute inferiority complex." It was also the inspiration for the Malvina Reynolds song about "little boxes made of ticky-tacky." True, most of its hills are covered with tracts that should have been torn down over fifty years ago. But the views from many of those homes are spectacular, stretching from the Pacific to the Bay. The downtown shopping area where Arthur Wight had his office isn't particularly attractive—mainly small stucco buildings with an amazing tangle of electrical and trolley bus wires overhead—and it doesn't help that quite often it's socked in by fog. But many people who live there love it for its lower home prices, relative peace and quiet, plentiful parking, and community services. Better than the city, especially for families with children.

I parked in the lot fronting Arthur Wight's suite, in a strip mall pretending to be an upscale office building. When I asked for Wight, the receptionist, who was sucking on a purple lollipop, jerked her thumb at me and said, "Back there."

And I'd thought *I* had employee problems!

Arthur Wight was a stocky little man; at first glance he reminded me of SpongeBob SquarePants. His brushy blond head was perched on his shoulders without discernible evidence of a neck. The rest of him, clad in a yellow-and-pink Hawaiian shirt and khaki shorts—in December, no less!—followed the same general body shape down to his knees, of which one was knobby and scarred, the other encased in a brace. He hobbled around his desk toward me, holding out his hand.

"Ms. McCone," he said, "sorry to meet you in such wretched shape. Please be warned not to take up skiing in your sixties." Then he motioned me to a chair.

"Actually," I told him, "I *did* take it up in my teens. A broken ankle on the bunny slope told me it was not my sport."

"You displayed good sense." He looked down at a file on the desk before him. "I understand you're here about last year's congressional hearings."

"Yes, I am. Someone connected with them may be making targets of me and my husband, Hy Ripinsky."

"In what way?"

I explained the attack on Elwood.

Wight leaned back in his chair, brow furrowed. "And you think I may be involved in that?"

"I don't know."

"No, you don't." Now he leaned forward. "I will tell you this, Ms. McCone, the arms dealing back then was the act of a young, stupid, wrongly idealistic young man. I was fortunate not to go to prison for my crimes. I'm sure that with your tech support, your agency can find out about all my activities since then, but let me tell you: I have never again strayed from the law. I've built up a reasonable practice here. No newsworthy or outstanding cases like yours or your colleagues'. A property-line dispute here, a child-custody case there. I've done a considerable amount of mediating: divorces, employer-employee conflicts, neighbors-versus-neighborhood-association disputes. Most of them were resolved to all parties' satisfaction. I've found that most people don't want to fight; they just don't want to be told what to do; they want to be left alone."

Amen to that.

I asked, "Are you still in touch with any of the—as you put it—young, stupid, and wrongly idealistic people you associated with?"

"No." He smiled cynically. "Those I know of are too busy improving their portfolios, golf scores, or real estate values." Now he leaned forward, hands clasped on the desk. "I'd like to emphasize, Ms. McCone, that I don't disapprove of any of their current choices. No one, no matter how dedicated or passionate about a cause, can nurse that flame forever. There's a rule about that: After ten years, it's starting to burn out. After twenty, it's gone."

I'd heard the same thing years before from a friend who was an EMT, and from another who was an undercover cop. So far I was still loving my work, and I hoped I would for many more years.

Another line of investigation closed.

11:15 a.m.

Derek had emailed me Don Taber's sketchy background information. He was a collector—read scavenger—of used automotive parts, many of which he found in trash cans. He would then refurbish and sell them at a tidy profit. His place of business, set back behind a high chain-link fence on El Camino Real, probably irked residents of the solidly middle-class, middle-income community. Most of them had been left out of the economic boom of Silicon Valley to the south, and the last thing they desired on their main thoroughfare was a lot containing a concrete-block office-and-shop combination and acres of car parts.

As I got out of my car, a sun-browned man in a Giants baseball cap greeted me. "What can I do for you, miss? Can't be you need a replacement for anything on that car—she's a beauty."

"Thank you. I'm looking for information on your report to the SFPD of a beaten man on Chestnut Street—"

"I didn't give my name. How'd you guys find me?"

If he wanted to assume I was a cop, that was all right with me. "When you call 911, your number appears on a screen so the dispatcher can call you back if the connection is broken."

"Well, I'll be damned."

"Could you describe what you witnessed in more detail?"

He folded his muscular arms across his chest, pursing his lips as he leaned against a fence post. "Well, it wasn't much. I was driving home from my daughter's place in Marin. I saw what I thought was a bunch of old clothes on the sidewalk in front of a store. A bum sleeping it off, I supposed. But then I saw he was moving around like he was hurt. That's when I got on the horn and called 911. You know, it takes forever to get in touch with them in your town."

I knew. Believe me, I knew.

"A long time for them to come out on a call too," he added. "I was concerned about the victim, so I parked across the street and watched. A few more minutes, I would've driven him to the hospital myself."

"Was anyone else in the vicinity when you first saw him?"

"No. Whoever beat him up was long gone."

"Why didn't you give the dispatcher your name?"

He just shrugged. But I already knew the answer. The standard old excuse: he hadn't wanted to get involved.

1:10 p.m.

Time for my meeting with Sylvia Blueflute.

Blueflute, a Hopi, Derek's fact sheet read, was short and plump, but with a manner that ensured no one would dare condescend to her because of her lack of stature. She greeted me in her office on the third floor of an elegant Victorian on Franklin Street and gave me coffee, and we settled into a comfortable conversation area in the corner turret. Through the wavy, rounded glass panes, I could see almost as much of an urban panorama as I could from my office window.

"Change and Growth is a co-op, right?" I asked.

"It is. This splendid house was left to us a number of years ago by a woman who was interested in Native rights, Alice Witherspoon. A number of us live, as well as maintain offices, here. Much like your All Souls Legal Cooperative was."

She'd done her homework.

"What happened to All Souls?" she asked.

I shrugged. "A faction came in, wanted to take it over, 'go downtown,' as they said. Most of us didn't agree with that, so we went elsewhere, leaving the dissident faction behind. Plus poverty law firms were on their way to becoming passé by then. I established my own agency, and I've never regretted it."

"And later the co-op dissolved?"

"Yes, amid a lot of bickering over what direction it would take."

"A loss."

I shrugged again. Maybe it was, maybe it wasn't. I'd been able to do far more with my own agency than I would have within the confines of the co-op.

"Ms. Blueflute," I said, "I understand you and your associates have extensive ties within the Indian community here."

"That's true."

"Do you gather information on what goes on within the community?"

"Not on a formal basis, but"—she grinned—"our spies are out there."

"Have there been any incidents of violence against Indians in the city recently?"

"Why are you asking? Because of the man who was found beaten and unconscious on Chestnut Street?"

"Yes. He's my father."

"Your father?"

"Does that surprise you?"

"Well...we get reports about incidents involving Native Americans from the police. But his name was different from yours. And he was described as being dressed in rags, while you—" She waved her hand at my suede jacket.

"My father is not into stylish clothes. He is, however, one of the foremost painters in the country."

"Painting...as in houses?"

"As in art."

"Oh." She paused, nibbling her lower lip. "How is he?"

"Still critical. You say you receive reports of crimes against Indians?"

"Native Americans."

"Are you correcting me, Ms. Blueflute?"

She flushed. "It's just that the term lends us so much more dignity—"

"To the heathens? Look, we could go on with this debate for hours, but I really don't have the time. So let's skip the semantics. I pretty much don't care about them, so long as our people get a fair deal. Now, have there been similar incidents recently?"

"A moment." She picked up her phone, dialed an extension, and spoke in a language that was completely foreign to me. Then she nodded, scribbling detailed notes on a legal pad.

"Yes, Ms. McCone," she said after she hung up. "There have been two. A woman named Samantha Killdeer was roughed up three weeks ago on Lombard Street—not the famous crooked part, but the block that rises from Van Ness. She's since given up her apartment and left town. An elderly man, Thomas Muniz, was mugged two months ago in the same area as your father; he succumbed to his injuries a few weeks later."

"Who was Mr. Muniz?"

"A janitor at Marina Middle School, on his way home to his room in the Mission. According to the police, he had no enemies and had committed no crimes."

"Except for being born of the wrong race. What else can you tell me about him and his attack?"

She flipped the pages of the pad in front of her. "A friendly man. A family man. He was seventy-one years old, and devoted to his grandchildren. He hadn't...well, done much with his life, but he was loved by all his relatives."

"When did his attack occur?"

"Around eleven thirty on a Friday night, at the intersection of Lombard and Van Ness."

"What was he doing there?"

"Waiting for the bus which would have deposited him a few blocks from his home."

"Had he been drinking?"

"His family swore he never took a drink, and the autopsy proved them out."

"Bad companions?"

"Not that anyone knew of."

"Drug use?"

"The autopsy said no."

Seemingly an open-and-shut case, but so many of them aren't.

I'd set my people on it, see what they could dredge up.

Blueflute stood, dismissing me. "My assistant will provide you with any further information you may need."

"I appreciate your talking with me," I said. "If you hear of any more incidents, please let me know."

2:01 p.m.

Blueflute had certainly made short work of our appointment, and I was fresh out of leads. I was just about to check in with Mick when he called.

"I've got the info on your painter," he said. "My friend at Cal says his name was Calvin Cook and he hailed from New

York City. He didn't know Elwood there, but admired his work enough to travel to St. Ignatius to try to meet him."

"You said his name *was*."

"He shot himself in an Oklahoma City motel room four years ago. He had mental issues and his work wasn't selling. He'd only had one show, in a downscale gallery in Coeur d'Alene, Idaho."

One more possible suspect eliminated.

"Well, thanks, Mick. Here's something else for you to check on." I told him of the murder of Thomas Muniz and the attack on Samantha Killdeer. He said he'd put someone on both right away.

2:33 p.m.

There was a message on my voice mail from Julia. She had talked to five residents of the three-story glass-and-chrome apartment building directly across the street from the site of the attack on Elwood, none of whom had seen anything. I drove over there and made contact with one more who had returned home since Julia's canvass. The matronly-looking woman had no knowledge of the attack.

Between two modern buildings was an architectural anomaly of a kind often found in the city: a narrow brick structure straight out of a Gothic novel. I was buzzed in by the first-floor tenant, a stooped old woman wearing a purple velvet sweat suit. One look at her cataract-clouded eyes told me she'd make a poor witness, but when I explained who I was and what I was after, she said, "So that was the commotion I heard. I couldn't see what was going on"—

she motioned at her eyes—"but my hearing is acute. The senses compensate. My name is Martha Daniels. Please come in."

She ushered me into her comfortable parlor and invited me to sit in a lounge chair.

I asked, "Do you mind if I record our conversation?"

"Not at all. Perhaps I might have a copy, something to amuse—and quiet—my noisy grandchildren when they come for Christmas?"

"Of course." I made a note on my pad. "You said there was a commotion?"

"Yes. I was sitting in this room, listening to an old radio program—*The Fred Allen Show*. You're too young to remember it, I assume."

"That particular one, yes. But my husband and I love those shows. We've got an old radio that's been modified for CDs, and we often listen to them in the dark."

She gave a hearty laugh. "In the dark, of course. That was the only way to listen to the mystery serials like *Lights Out* and *The Whistler*. They could scare the pants off you. Anyway, the noise in the street was loud. Stamping footsteps—hard heels, you know? A collective rumble of voices, as if a riot were starting. Sounds of blows. I should have had my phone with me so I could call 911, but for some reason I'd left it in the kitchen."

"And then?"

"I started to get up and locate it, when there was a shout. A man yelled, 'Come on, guys, let's get outta here.' And they ran."

"Would you recognize the man's voice if you heard it again?"

"I certainly would. As I said before, the senses compensate."

2:55 p.m.

Martha Daniels had told me that many of the other residents of her building worked at home, so to spare them
an interruption, I saved them for later and went on to the
next—an undistinguished modern three-story pile with too
much glass and peeling trim and bars on the lower-floor
windows. To keep intruders out or the tenants in?

Probably the latter; anyone who would choose to live in
such a dump must be insane.

*A snob, McCone, that's what you've turned into. Consider
some of the places* you've *lived.*

Well, yeah...

My college residences had consisted of a series of small
apartments—no, call them rat holes—in which any number of indigent students crashed from time to time. My
primary reason for getting into the security business was
that it was easier to study at night while guarding mostly
empty office buildings than in places where loud music,
parties, and personal crises might erupt at any moment.
Hank Zahn had solved that problem by inviting me to live
for my last two years in a big old house he and several
others rented close to the UC campus. Sure, there were
loud music, parties, and personal crises, but there were
also civility and respect for each other's privacy, and no
crashers were allowed. Still, I was happy when I graduated
and was done with communal living. My studio apartment

on Guerrero Street in the Mission wasn't a step up, but it was mine alone. My house on nearby Church Street was a handyman's nightmare, but fortunately I'm handy, and so are a number of my friends and associates in the building trades…

I stopped reminiscing and started up the building's steps.

It looked to have four apartments to a floor. There was no response at the first three apartments I buzzed, but I received an answering buzz from the fourth. I went through the door into a maroon-carpeted hallway that smelled strongly of mildew.

"Over here," a male voice called. "You the new therapist?"

"Uh, no. Are you expecting one?"

"Yeah, but I should've known you weren't her. Therapists're never on time." The man stepped out into the hallway. A big curly-haired black man on crutches, wearing a blue bathrobe.

I exclaimed, "You're Traynor McManus!" McManus had been a star interior line player with the 49ers until he sustained a severe spinal injury.

He inclined his head. "Thank you for remembering me, miss."

"And thank *you* for not calling me 'ma'am'—makes me feel like my mother." I handed him my card and explained who I was; he ushered me into his front room, which was equipped with two leather Barcaloungers and one of the largest flat-screen TVs I'd ever seen.

"Sit, please," he said while lowering himself into what was obviously his favorite chair. A table sat on either side of it, both covered with books and DVDs; the table next to my chair held nothing but a lamp.

He saw me looking at it and said, "It's what happens in a weak marriage when the star stops being one."

"I'm sorry—"

He waved my words away. "Was over two years ago. I've acclimated. No kids involved, thank God. Actually the whole mess has opened new worlds to me." He motioned at the books and DVDs. "So much fascinating stuff out there that it's hard to decide what or who I want to be when I grow up. So what brings you here today? Not my faded fame."

"No, but meeting you is an unexpected pleasure. Actually, I'm canvassing the neighborhood for witnesses to an assault that happened on Tuesday between midnight and two a.m. on the other side of the street."

McManus scrutinized my card. "The old guy who was beaten by a gang of thugs, right?"

"Yes."

"News said he was an Indian, same as the Muniz man."

"Correct."

He peered more keenly at me. "And you've got a vested interest in the crime. You related to him?"

"His daughter."

"Thought so." He flipped the card between his fingers. "I've heard of you, you know. You get decent press. And I want to help you. I didn't see or hear anything; my bed-room's at the rear. But I can steer you to people who might have."

I took out my recorder and asked his permission to turn it on.

McManus held up a cautioning hand. "I don't want my name associated with this, and I want you to be very careful.

A few of these people are just plain mean. And you never know about the others."

"I can read people well, and usually I know when to keep my big mouth shut."

He smiled and began naming quite a list, labeling them B, L, or N: bigot, liberal, or neutral.

"For somebody who doesn't get out a lot, you know a lot about quite a few of your neighbors," I said.

"Oh yeah. I'm the local celebrity. Women bring me pies and casseroles. Men want to talk 'real football' with me. Frankly, I wish the guys would stay in front of their TVs and the women would romance me."

McManus was a talented athlete who'd had his shot at fame, but would never play again. And he wasn't bitter. Sad a lot of the time, I suspected, but he'd put what happened in perspective. Given his poise, good looks, and deep voice, I wouldn't be surprised to see him on TV doing commentary on the NFL games one of these days.

3:25 p.m.

I started with the L's on McManus's list. Members of the liberal community were more likely to be comfortable with the nature of my inquiry. McManus had starred a few names, and one—Yvonne Grace—lived on the second floor of his building. When I pushed her doorbell, a husky voice called out, "Come on in!"

Trusting woman, in a building with so little security.

The walls of the narrow hallway I entered were hung with masks: some looked to be African, others Asian; some were ceramic, some papier-mâché. As I passed between them toward the source of the woman's voice, they all seemed to view me dourly.

The woman herself appeared in a spotlight-filled room at the end of the hall. She was tall, with pale-blonde hair wrapped in a braid that was supposed to curl around the top of her head; unfortunately, the plait had slipped and was in danger of resting atop her left ear. Black paint and clay-stained sweats completed her ensemble.

"Oh, don't mind them," she said, gesturing at the masks, "they glare at me all the time too."

"Then why do you keep them?"

"I don't—for very long. They're my livelihood, and I sell 'em as fast as I can. Don't know why people want such evil creatures. Maybe to remind them of their own evildoing?"

"Or maybe to remind them of the evil that's been done to them." I held out one of my cards. "I'm—"

"Sharon McCone. Tray called to say you'd probably be around." She led me into the light-filled room, where the floor was covered with a tarp and a rose-colored sofa was encased in plastic.

"May I offer you something?" she asked. "Coffee or tea?"

"No, thanks. I'm good for now."

"That's a relief. My pantry's *not* good; I think I used the last teabag twice." She flopped down on the other end of the sofa. "I'm working on this huge commission for a Cinco de Mayo celebration down in LA. Dozens of individually crafted masks, and you wouldn't expect that it would take me until May to deliver, but I'm barely on schedule as is."

"I'll try not to take up much of your time."

"You won't. Uncle Tray—he's not really my uncle, but that's what everybody calls him—told me what you're after. I was working late in the studio when the attack happened"—she motioned toward a portion of the room that was partitioned off by plywood—"and didn't see or hear a thing. However, I do sense that something's going down in this area that's not good."

"What kind of something?"

"It's hard to pin down, just a feeling I have."

"Other assaults?"

"Well, there was a Native American named Thomas Muniz who was attacked not long ago—"

"Yes, I know about that. It may or may not be related."

"Well, maybe I'm just imagining things. I've always been hypersensitive to my environment."

I showed her the list Traynor had given me. "You know any of these people?"

She studied it. "Some. What's this coding mean—L, N, and B?"

"Liberal, neutral, and bigoted."

"Uncle Tray's creation, I suppose. Well, he's got it down right. I'd put this one"—she picked up a pen from a side table and made a check mark—"into the neutral category. And this one"—another check—"is as bigoted as they get. But you know, Sharon, people aren't just going to reveal their prejudices to you. You're going to have to play the 'my poor daddy' card."

"Oh, I will. You bet I will."

4:01 p.m.

Yvonne and I had gone over the list of names, ordering them by priority. Of course, I wanted to go up against the worst of the bigots first, but I accepted her insider's wisdom and decided to start with the L's.

I sat down on the building's steps and checked with SFG. Elwood's condition was stable, a positive sign even though he still hadn't regained consciousness. Then I connected with Saskia and Robin, who were keeping their vigil at the hospital. Hy's phone was turned off—a situation that always makes me twitchy.

Since it was late in the afternoon, I headed back to the office. Traffic was wicked as usual, with jams in unpredictable places and a crash that blocked my freeway exit and sent me out of my way. I was thoroughly out of sorts when I arrived.

I grew even more agitated when I saw a crowd on the sidewalk blocking access to the main entry. Media people with cameras and microphones, and a TV van that was interfering with traffic. What on earth were they doing here?

I slipped around the TV van and drove into our underground parking lot. From there I took the stairs to the lobby. One of our security guards, Ken Rand, was standing at his post, beefy arms folded across his chest.

"Ms. McCone," he exclaimed, "am I glad you're here! They seem to be looking for you. I locked the doors, but they won't go away."

"Isn't there anything we can do about them?"

"I've tried. *Really* tried. But they're on a public sidewalk."

"And creating a public nuisance. If they get out of hand, call the cops."

Upstairs, Ted greeted me, looking upset. "I think we'd better sit down someplace private."

With rising apprehension I led him back to my office. "What?" I asked.

"A story about you being Elwood's daughter broke on the early news. This place has been a madhouse ever since."

"Damn! How did they find out?"

"You know the media—they just keep digging and digging until they come up with something. We've been frantic, shooing reporters away. They're making a big deal of it."

"Why?"

"Maybe it's a slow news day?" He smiled when he spoke, but his face was grave.

"Where's Ripinsky?"

"Off in some other world, as far as I can tell. He's in his office with that look on his face—you know the one I mean—as if he were catatonic."

Oh yes—I knew that look. It meant he was struggling with a problem, working at a solution. I'd watched him many a time: he'd sit like stone, then the muscles of his face would begin to move. A tic by one eye; a twitch of his lips; an "Uh-huh" deep in his throat. His eyes would blink and he'd say, "I've got it, McCone." And usually he had.

"Don't disturb him," I told Ted, even though he didn't need to be reminded. "Alert me when he returns to planet Earth."

Minutes later a high-pitched shriek came from somewhere in the suite, loud enough to penetrate the closed door to my office. I jumped up, ran down the hall; other people were gathering in front of a closet where we kept cleaning supplies. Ted had apparently gotten there first, and he was picking up from the floor a small, quivering person in a gray uniform whom I recognized as one of our regular cleaning staff. I pushed through the others and went to her.

When she realized I was there she said, "Oh, Sharon, it was awful! He was hiding in there, and when I opened the door he took my picture."

"Who?"

"A guy I saw with those reporters Ted's been running off. He must've hid in the closet."

I turned to Ted. "You know who he is?"

Ted asked the housekeeper, "Can you describe him?"

"He was sort of funny looking. Short and round with a bald head and thick glasses."

"Dean Abbot," Ted said. "One of the prominent members of our lunatic fringe."

Well, that figured. "Did he hurt you?" I asked the woman.

"No. Just scared the hell out of me."

"Where did he go?"

She shrugged. "Don't know."

"Okay, I think you should go home for the rest of the day, take it easy."

She gave me a little smile and went down the hallway to the coat closet. I noticed that she opened the door gingerly and peeked inside before she got her jacket.

Dean Abbot—the name was familiar. I asked Ted, "How do you know him?"

"I thought everybody did. He's a high-end techie called King of the Blogs. He's got about a dozen of them."

"What does he write about?"

"Whatever. Today, one of them, it was all about tooth-brushes."

"What the hell can you say about toothbrushes?"

"Damned if I know. I didn't read it."

"Can you—"

"Get some more info on him? Yes, I can."

"What do you suppose he was doing here?"

"Probably trying to get a look at our computer system. What I didn't get around to telling you yet—Dean Abbot is known as one of the best hackers in the West."

"Better than Mick?"

"Hey, baby—nobody's better than Mick."

I hoped.

5:10 p.m.

Our security staff had investigated and found that Dean Abbot was nowhere on the premises. I called our attorney to ask about legal remedies, but the firm's offices were closed until after the holiday. Then I did paperwork until Hy appeared in my office about the time I decided to call it a day. There was more paperwork to tend to, documents and checks to sign, but I'd about had it by then.

"Was a mess out there, right?" he said.

"Yeah. For a few minutes I felt as if I'd been thrown to the lions."

"Has Elwood regained consciousness yet?"

"Not yet. The hospital would have let me know if he had."

"The sooner he does the better. I have a lot of questions to ask him."

"What questions?"

"His impressions of the attack. The old five senses, you

know: visual images, odors, what he felt other than pain, what he heard. Did he fight back, maybe mark one of them? Did he realize what direction they were coming from? What, if anything, made them stop beating him?"

"You really expect him to have noticed anything in the middle of a vicious assault?"

"Yes, I do. Because I have."

"Ripinsky, he's an old man—"

"A shrewd old man who's finely tuned into the world. Aren't you the one who always deplores the way our country infantilizes older people?"

"Okay, I was guilty of faulty thinking. But he's my *father*."

"All the more reason to trust whatever recollections he might have. You didn't get all your intuition from your mother."

"Certainly not. Saskia deals in facts, solid evidence."

"But it takes intuition to piece them all together. You got your gift from both sides."

"So what's this so-called gift supposed to be telling me now? You're the one who's spent his day in quiet contemplation."

"What we need to find out first of all: is it only a hate crime against Indians, or other minority groups as well?"

"Other Indians have been crime victims recently." I relayed what I'd learned about Muniz and Killdeer. "Muniz has died, and Killdeer moved away, no forwarding. There's sure a lot of hate going around these days. And it's not all coming from Caucasians. Everybody's got an agenda, and the hate is usually directed at some group that we think has a hate on for us."

"Everybody? Sure. Who do you hate?" Hy said.

I thought for a moment. "Violent criminals, people who prey on children, people who take advantage of the elderly, scammers of all kinds, insurance companies and their inflated rates, Big Pharma that soaks people who need their medicines to survive, drug pushers and addicts, sexual predators of all types, animal abusers, most politicians—"

"You see? Hate is a common commodity. Do you know the word appeared in two front-page headlines in the *Chron* today?"

"Yeah, I saw it. So is what was done to Elwood a simple hate crime? If so, are the perps—I'm assuming more than one because one person couldn't have administered so much damage—an organized group? White, Hispanic, black, Islamic? Are there cells of such people in the city? Or are they only bad boys who were out on the town and spotted somebody who they thought didn't belong? Have they done this before? Were they simply drunks from the bars and, if so, what set them off?"

"That's a lot of questions covering a lot of territory."

"I suggest we find out about organized groups in the area. I can put Mick and Derek on that. Roberta can cover the bars, ask if any rowdy bunch was in late that night."

"And you and I?"

"Later on tonight, we'll walk the streets of the Marina, have something to eat, see what we can pick up on."

9:10 p.m.

The evening was very dark when Hy and I went for our walk. No one was out and about on Avila Street, and we saw few people except for fanatical joggers as we made our way to Chestnut, the main—and very chic—shopping area for the district. We'd debated how to dress for our outing: wear our usual clothing, or opt for downscale, as Elwood had? Finally we'd decided we'd be less conspicuous and possibly learn more if we looked as if we belonged. Both of us were armed: Hy with his .45, me with my .38. We walked closely together without entwining arms or hands, spoke sparingly and in low voices.

I said, "That's the jewelry store where Elwood was found. Jesus, I can still see blood spots in the doorway."

"No, you can't. There's not enough light."

"Okay, so I'm imagining it."

We stepped up to the store to look through the display window. "Those aquamarine earrings," I said. "He knows I love that color."

"And the watches—the day he arrived, he commented on how shabby mine was. Asked if it was reliable."

"So he was looking for presents for us. That makes me feel really terrible."

"Not your fault that your father cares for us."

"Still…"

"I know."

We turned away from the window and walked on. There were more people on the sidewalks here, window-shopping or going in and out of the area's many restaurants. They chattered in groups, blocking other pedestrians, walked without looking where they were going. An obviously drunken man was singing "Here Comes Sanna Claus"; his companions were trying without success to shut him up.

My cell vibrated and I stepped into a doorway to answer it. Roberta Cruz, our newest operative.

"Shar, I'm in a bar called the Twenty-Second Century on Chestnut near Scott Street. The bartender says there was a pretty unpleasant group in here the night Mr. Farmer was attacked, voicing racist sentiments."

I looked around, spotted the bar half a block from us. "Be there shortly. Keep him talking."

We hurried over there. Roberta was hunched over on a barstool, talking with a bald-headed man with thick, black-framed glasses. She smiled when she saw us, her rather homely, elongated face lighting up. When Roberta smiled, it could brighten even the dingiest room.

The Twenty-Second Century was your standard neighborhood hangout: a long bar with stools; six booths upholstered in red plastic; retro checkerboard black-and-white tiles. It wasn't as chic as most other drinking establishments in the Marina, but it had a welcoming ambiance that many of them didn't. The few customers looked up and smiled as Hy and I came in.

Roberta motioned us over. "This is Mr. Charley Willingham, the owner and bartender," she said, and gave him our names.

We sat down and ordered drinks. I asked him if I could record our conversation, and he agreed. But before we got around to discussing what Mr. Willingham had to tell us, he said, "The place is for sale. At a good price too. I inherited it two years ago from my uncle, and I've been trying to sell it ever since. Don't have the temperament to run a business. But the bar's profitable, the location's good, the regular clientele are nice. You'd think, given the prices people're getting for absolute dumps in this city, that someone would've made an offer by now."

Willingham was not a person who could easily be held to a subject. However, you can also learn unexpected things from people who ramble.

"About the group who came in...," I said.

"Oh yeah. It was about forty-five minutes before closing on the night—well, actually the morning—the old man was attacked." He nodded to me. "Five of them, and they'd been having a high time, but I didn't think it was enough of one to refuse service. A bartender has to exercise discretion, you know. Moderately high, okay. No tension among them, nobody being loud—that's okay too. Language, well, that's discretionary. Me, I don't like the f-bomb, but it's pretty common these days, even with women. If you ask me, broads have filthier mouths than the guys sometimes."

He winked at me and plunged onward. "What happened was, they took that booth over there"—he motioned to my right—"and for a while everything was fine. But then I was clearing out the booth next to them, and I heard what they were talking about." He shook his head. "Some of the ugliest talk ever."

"What did they say?" I asked.

"Racist stuff. You know: nigger, wop, Injun, slant, Jew-boy—you name it, they used it. I don't usually interfere with the customers' conversations, but I did ask them to turn down the volume. They lowered it for a while. Then they got loud again and one of them said, 'Hey, there's the old man now. Let's go get him.' That's when they left—trying not to pay their tab. I nailed one of them, and he forked over."

"'Let's go get him.' *Who*? Somebody they knew?"

"Sounded like they'd seen him before. Maybe were waiting for him."

I took a deep breath before asking, "Can you describe them?"

"Young, college age or a little older. Short hair, but not like the neo-Nazis wear. All of them white, of course. Nicely dressed. Expensive-looking jewelry, but none of this bling you see on pro athletes. One of them had a watch that could've been one of those new Apples."

"And you'd never seen them before?"

"No."

"Could you identify them if you saw them again?"

"I sure could."

"Was there anyone in the group who stood out, seemed to be the leader?"

He thought about it. "Yeah. The guy with the Apple. He was maybe older than the others, and they all kind of deferred to him. I heard somebody call him Jersey—you know, as in the state."

"What did this Jersey look like?"

"Tall, maybe six three. Skinny. Don't know about hair color—he had a Giants baseball cap on the whole time."

"Eye color?"

"He wore shades, even inside and at night."

"Any identifying marks? Tattoos?"

"No. Wore a Giants jacket too, and he kept it on."

Giants fan. Affluent enough to buy an Apple Watch. No identifying marks.

Not much to go on.

"A couple more questions, Mr. Willingham. When did you hear of the attack on Elwood Farmer?"

"The morning after. I was setting up in here, and the neighbor runs that motel down the block came in and told me."

"And why didn't you report what you just told me to the police?"

Behind his thick glasses, Willingham's eyes widened. "Go to the cops? Why?"

"Because the more time that elapses between a crime and a person's probable knowledge of it, the less likely it'll be solved."

"I didn't have any definite knowledge a crime was gonna be committed. Besides, I can't afford to get involved in stuff like that."

That old excuse again. "I'm afraid you're already involved, Mr. Willingham." I held up my recorder. "You consented to me using this."

9:51 p.m.

"Well, that shut him up," Roberta whispered as the owner turned away to serve another customer.

"Tape recorders usually do," I told her. "So what do we have? Five men, their leader a tall, thin guy called Jersey wearing a Giants cap and jacket, sunglasses, and maybe an Apple Watch."

"More than we had before," Hy said.

"Right. Our best lead so far."

Roberta said hesitantly, "Willingham's a talker, but he seems pretty sharp. What if we got that sketch artist you've used before—Rob Lewis—to work with him?"

"Good idea," I said, "if Willingham will go for it."

"I'll find out." She motioned to Willingham, spoke softly to him.

I said to Hy, "She's amazing—from the way that he's bobbing his head, she has him wrapped around her little finger."

Roberta gave a thumbs-up sign, then turned back to Willingham. I guessed that she was explaining to him about Rob Lewis and his Identi-Kit.

I phoned Rob Lewis. He was home, and when I explained the situation, he agreed to a meeting with Willingham. He couldn't do it the next day because of another commitment. He suggested two o'clock on Friday afternoon.

"It's set for Friday," I called.

Willingham and Roberta came over to our booth. He said, "Bertie here has explained how important this stuff is, and I'm happy to help. Frankly, it scares me that there're so many of these vicious animals going around pretending to be human. And they're not always what you expect. They look respectable, could be any of us, except that something's been left out of them. Sympathy, empathy, whatever you want to call it."

"My mother would've said their hearts're empty," Roberta said.

Willingham replied, "I just say it's a tragedy—for them and for the people they hurt."

FRIDAY, DECEMBER 22

9:18 a.m.

The first thing I did when I arrived at M&R was to call Sergeant Anders. She had nothing new to report. I told her about the five young men who'd been making racist comments in the Twenty-Second Century.

"Their leader is apparently named Jersey. Tall, thin, a Giants fan—wears a cap and jacket with the team's logo, as well as an expensive watch. Ring any bells?"

"No. But I'll see if we have anything on him in our files and let you know."

On my way down the hallway to my office I went in to see Derek and gave him the same information. "Giants caps and jackets and flash jewelry are all over the city these days," he said. "But Jersey's not a common name, even as a nickname. I'll see if I can dig up anything."

In my office I buzzed Patrick, who had recently taken over the scheduling of our operatives, and asked him to make sure one or more of them would night-patrol the area where Elwood was attacked, and keep an eye on the Twenty-Second Century in case the predators showed up again.

"Sure. I'll put a friend on it for tonight."

"Is he qualified?"

Patrick laughed. "He's a former San Jose cop—five years on the force. He moved north when his marriage broke up, and has been filling in at various jobs with agencies since last summer. Is that qualified enough for you?"

"More than."

I spent the rest of the morning on the usual paperwork. I was trying to transfer much of my administrative work to Ted; he in turn had been trying to turn his over to anyone who would have it. As a result the M&R work flow resembled a backed-up sewer pipe. Not a very nice way to refer to our clients and their problems, but that was what I visualized when I thought about it.

As I passed Roberta's desk on my way to fetch more coffee, I said, "Hi, Bertie. Good work last night."

"Sssh!" She put a finger to her lips and flushed. "Thanks, Shar. But cut the 'Bertie' stuff—it's a kid nickname I use as a kind of alias when I don't want people to know how to find me. You know—people like Willingham."

"I know. Believe me, I know."

"Hey, McCone," Hy said, stepping out of my office. I hadn't yet talked with him this morning, since he'd been in the shower when I left. "Anything to report?"

"Nothing further from the hospital. I put Derek onto locating the racist trash-talker called Jersey."

"It's a start, anyway."

I told him about the patrol duty in the Marina. Hy thought it was good idea too. Then he said, "I was wondering: this woman you spoke with who makes the masks—did she seem reliable to you?"

"Well, her claims to feeling something's wrong in the neighborhood don't have any definite basis."

"But there *are* people with heightened senses. Look at you and me: from the very first we've shared a psychic connection—and a damn hard one to break. During that confidential case I handled for the FBI up near the Canadian border, I had to work like the devil to shut you out."

"True."

"And some of the connections you make in your investigations defy reason, but they're mostly correct."

"So you're saying I should open myself to the 'vibes' around me?"

Hy smiled. "Sounds very sixties, doesn't it? But I've got no new jargon to replace it."

"Well, the idea has validity. Not *everybody* was stoned out of their minds back then."

The phone rang, interrupting us. I picked up without checking to see who was calling.

"Don't hang up on me," a deep, familiar voice said.

Glenn Solomon, one of the city's premier criminal defense attorneys and my former friend until he put my life at stake by withholding critical information in an investigation.

"Why shouldn't I?"

"Because I am calling to atone—and you know how difficult that is for me. Besides, Bette sends her love."

Bette Silver, Glenn's wife, an outstanding interior designer who had done much of the work on our house.

"I send mine back to her."

"I am sorry, deeply sorry, for the situation I put you in. And as part of my atonement, I wish to offer my services."

"To do what?"

"I'd rather do this in person. Can you come to my office? Or I'll come to yours."

"I'll be at yours in forty-five minutes."

10:41 a.m.

Embarcadero Center has long been a fixture on the San Francisco skyline, a complex of five office towers, many commercial establishments, and two hotels on a four-block area between the financial and waterfront districts. Glenn's offices were in Embarcadero Four, the tallest in the complex at forty-five floors, and—wouldn't you know it?—on the top floor.

Glenn was a big, burly man with a thick shock of white hair, impeccably attired in a custom-tailored gray suit and elegant tie. Although he had to be in his seventies, his face was as smooth as a baby's. I'd long wanted to peek behind his ears for the telltale suture marks of a facelift, but now I decided that would be overstepping the boundaries of our former friendship. Or maybe new friendship, as it seemed to be on again.

I let him hug me, after which he steered me to one of a pair of comfortable armchairs.

I said, "I'm surprised to hear from you."

"I'm here to catch up, now that all the hoopla's ended."

"What hoopla?"

"Last week Hanukkah began. Bette and I don't really celebrate it, but she does light the menorah. I've strayed a long way from my Jewish faith, but at this time of year something

touches me in a way I can't explain. Makes me want to connect with people I've slighted or hurt. This year, mainly you.
I've been following your latest case on the Internet; it's com-
pelling, because the kind of people you're battling are the
same type who herded my people into cattle cars less than a
hundred years ago."

I was touched, but I didn't know what to say.

Glenn went on, "I understand, from sources I can't reveal,
that you are wading into potentially dangerous waters. The
groups in this city who organize to promote bigotry are extremely retaliatory and vicious."

"My father—"

"I know about the incident. How is he doing?"

"There's been a little improvement in his condition, but
not as much yet as we hoped for."

"Would you like a second opinion? I could send in my
own doctor."

"That's not necessary, but thanks for offering."

Glenn pulled a legal pad in front of him and began to
write. In a moment he tore off the top sheet and pushed it
toward me. "Talk to this woman. She has her finger on the
pulse of the city and may be able to help you."

"Okay to give your name as a reference?"

"Of course. In fact, I'll call her and tell her to expect to
hear from you."

12:30 p.m.

Cynthia Sharpe, the woman Glenn had referred me to, was
willing to see me at her Pacific Heights mansion—she ac-

tually called it a mansion—if I arrived at twelve thirty. The Spanish colonial house on California Street was in total confusion when I arrived: caterers' and florists' trucks clogged the street; men were erecting Christmas lights in the front yard and shouting. Inside it was more of a melee: servers carrying trays and bashing into each other; frantic men on ladders trying to trim one of the most enormous Christmas trees I'd ever seen. And in the midst of all this on a pale-green sofa sat Cynthia Sharpe in a yellow silk lounging suit, surveying the workers with a bemused smile and sipping a glass of champagne.

She snapped at one of the workmen, then rose and extended her hand to me. Apparently I was a rung up from the hired help—but she didn't offer me any champagne.

"Please sit down, Ms. McCone," she said. "These holiday benefits are a pain to put on, but they do so help the orphans."

"The orphans?"

"Indian children, deprived of their families." She studied me, her eyes narrowed. "Do you have Indian blood yourself?"

"Yes. Shoshone."

"I don't believe I know much about that particular tribe."

"We're very peaceable. The most notable thing we've done was introduce the horse to the other tribes in the Old West."

"Interesting." She drank more champagne, then added briskly, "Glenn Solomon said you need information for one of your cases."

"Yes. My father, Elwood Farmer, was severely beaten on Chestnut Street in the Marina district early last Tuesday morning. Apparently his attackers were a group of affluent-looking whites who were overheard making racial slurs in a nearby bar beforehand. Glenn thought you might be able to shed light on their identities."

"I? For heaven's sake, why?"

"He didn't say. Perhaps because of your commitment to the Indian orphans."

With an airy wave of her hand, she dismissed a goodly portion of my people. "Oh, that. You know how it is with charities in this town, Ms. McCone. Unless you're a true do-gooder or high up on the social ladder, you take what you can get. I ended up with Indian orphans."

My spine stiffened, but I kept my face emotionless. "Do you know any of these orphans, Ms. Sharpe?"

"Oh, there'll be a couple of them at the fund-raiser, cleaned up and dressed decently."

"But you don't actually *know* any of them."

She frowned. "Why should I?"

"What about members of hate groups?"

"Members of what?"

"Groups of people who organize to do Indians or other minorities harm."

"Why would I...?" She paused. "Well, there *is* Rolle."

"R-o-l-l-y?"

"No, with an *e*. Rolle Ferguson, of the Atherton Fergusons."

"Important people?"

Ms. Sharpe widened her eyes as if surprised I hadn't heard of them. "Oh my, yes. Rolle's great-grandfather established the First Pacific National Bank and Trust. The family went on into other lucrative business ventures."

"Why did you mention him?"

"He has very conservative views. And often protests racially sensitive causes."

"Such as?"

"Well…when he was in high school, he picketed his class's junior prom because the king and queen were an interracial couple."

"What else has he protested?"

"Affirmative action programs. Amnesty for undocumented immigrants. A Black Lives Matter rally."

"Anything to do with Indians? Orphan relief funding, for instance?"

"Yes. That too."

"Have any of his protests been violent?"

"Not to my knowledge."

"Has he ever been in trouble with the law?"

"I have no idea."

"What else can you tell me about him?"

"That's all, I'm afraid. Now if you'll excuse me, Ms. McCone, I have a great many things that require my attention."

Right. Such as another glass of champagne.

1:32 p.m.

The first thing I did when I got back to my car was call Mick. "I have a possible lead," I said. "There's a man named Rolle Ferguson—that's r-o-l-l-e—of the Atherton Fergusons. A woman I interviewed today mentioned him. He has a background of protests that mark him as a bigot."

"The violent kind?"

"Ms. Sharpe didn't know. See what you can find out about him and his activities."

"Will do. Oh, and Derek told me to pass on the nonnews that he hasn't been able to find out anything yet about the guy called Jersey."

"Okay. Talk to you later."

I broke the connection and phoned Priscilla Anders at the SFPD. She had nothing to report to me either. There was nothing in the department's files or the CJIS pertaining to anyone known as Jersey. I considered giving her Rolle Ferguson's name, but decided to wait until I had more information about the man.

Before I returned to the agency, I detoured to SFG for another check on Elwood's condition. Ma was in the small waiting room, curled up sound asleep on the sofa. Nobody else was there, but Ma was stubborn enough to want to keep a continual vigil.

Dr. Stiles wasn't available, but one of the nurses told me Elwood had spent a restless night. This was not necessarily a bad sign; it might mean he was starting to come out of the coma. I sat with my father a while. He was not restless now; in fact, he looked as if he were carved out of wax.

My father...How easily I accepted Elwood now. But for a long time I'd fought the notion, perhaps because I'd loved my adoptive father very much. Andrew McCone. A big man, with a full head of white hair and a ruddy face. A former chief with the US Navy who, after his retirement at thirty years, had devoted his time to woodworking and puttering around the house singing dirty ditties. He'd died at his workbench in the cluttered garage of our old San Diego house, putting together a small box made of finely cut pieces of exotic woods; I'd finished it myself, and today it stands on a special table—also Pa's work—in my living room. Miraculously, both of these precious items had survived the fire when my house on Church Street burned to the ground, and I'd been able to restore the smoke damage.

In a way, I thought now, Pa and Elwood were much alike: both artists, although in different ways; both easygoing and good natured; both with a sly sense of humor. I'd married a man much like them, except there was an edge to Hy, which complemented my own edge. Where I'd gotten that I wasn't sure. Maybe from Saskia.

I smiled as I thought of the elk horn–framed photograph Elwood had presented me with upon my first visit to him: Saskia, my great-aunt Fenella, and others whom Fenella had met on a visit to the reserve the year before I was born. Although Elwood had had no idea I was his daughter when I visited, some feeling must have stirred him, because the photo was a treasured possession. When my Church Street house was the victim of arson, the photo fortunately had been out on loan to the Native Americans' Museum for a special exhibition, and thus saved. It now resides on our mantelpiece.

After about fifteen minutes, I kissed Elwood on the cheek and went on to the office.

2:15 p.m.

I checked in with the few staff members who were there. Julia was planning a surveillance on a jewelry store in the Mission that had twice been broken into; her strategy was to leave open the window they'd previously entered by, turn off the newly installed alarm, and wait for the would-be thieves to return. "I know the Mission punks," she told me. "They'll be back. And the cops aren't going to be any help; crime in the Mission isn't a priority."

Sad but true. All too often, manpower and muscle follow the money.

Patrick, whom we'd jokingly named the head of our deadbeat dad division, was chasing down one in Pacifica, south of the city. He hated deadbeat dads with a passion because he was raising his two sons alone after their mother abandoned the family. I left him a note asking that he get in touch with me.

When I came out of Patrick's office I noticed that there was a strange person at our reception desk. Strange in that I didn't know him—not strange meaning bizarre. He saw me, rose, and extended his hand.

"Ms. McCone," he said, "I'm Jason Lieberman, from ProTemp Services. Mr. Smalley asked that they send someone to help out here during the staff shifts."

What staff shifts?

I extended my hand. His grasp was firm, his fingers stained with what looked to be ink from a black cartridge.

He saw me looking at it and said, "It won't come off on you. I know, because I've been scrubbing at it for two days." His eyes twinkled and he added, "They're out to get us, you know."

"Who?"

"The ink cartridge companies. They want to damage our appearances so we won't rise on the corporate ladder."

Maybe Jason *was* bizarre, or maybe…?

"You're a friend of Ted's, right?"

"Yes, I am."

"Well, that explains it. Carry on."

I skirted the desk and went down the hall to Mick's office. "What's the deal with Jason?"

"Kendra quit, so at Ted's suggestion I called ProTemp and asked for him."

"Kendra quit? Why?"

"She wouldn't say, but I think it's that she's having trouble coping with both the job and that family of hers." He shook his head.

Kendra Williams had a large family at home, none of whom seemed capable of managing anything alone. Their parents were both dead, and they demanded her services as chief cook, cleaner, and caregiver. Yet she always tried to pick up the slack here, staying late while issuing familial orders by phone: *The dryer is* not *busted; try cleaning the lint trap...Use Resolve, not Windex, on the carpet...Three hundred and fifty degrees is what you cook the casserole at...Give the cat her hairball medicine...Don't give Missy the red pills! They could kill her. Hers are the blue ones.*

All of this delivered in a pleasant modulated tone—well, except when someone was about to administer a potentially lethal overdose.

Her calm, steady hand was one of the many reasons I didn't want to lose Kendra. And her family's financial needs couldn't be met without us. Something needed to be done. But what? And how? Kendra was proud; she'd never accept charity.

I said, "Let's all of us try to think of a creative solution to this problem. Kendra badly needs her salary and benefits, and it'd be nearly impossible to replace her."

"I'll spread the word around," Mick agreed.

"Good. Do you have those files on the hate crimes yet?"

"They're on your desk. I know you don't like to read off the computer for long periods, so I printed them out. Grim stuff. The file only reveals a small part of what's going on with the hate groups, here and nationwide. Makes me never want to leave this high-security building again."

"Ugly stuff, huh?"

"Some of the ugliest."

"I can hardly wait. Have you or Derek gotten any information on the Jersey person?"

"Nothing on Jersey."

"What about Rolle Ferguson and his family?"

"His mother and father used to be pillars of Atherton society, lived on a big estate down there. They're both dead now—an aviation accident in Europe."

"And Rolle?"

"He's the black sheep. He angered his parents with his stances on racial discrimination and abortion issues. According to friends, they were about to cut him out of their will when their small plane went down in the Swiss Alps. Rolle inherited the whole shebang."

"Consisting of?"

"The Atherton property, a summer home at Lake Tahoe, and a condo in Pacific Heights."

"Where in Pacific Heights?"

"Divisidero Street. Down near Cow Hollow."

That address was only a few blocks across Lombard Street from the Marina—an indication that Rolle Ferguson might have been involved in the attacks on Elwood, Muniz, and Killdeer.

Mick went on, "Rolle also inherited cash accounts, an art collection, a small yacht, and a couple of expensive cars."

"No corporations?"

"Ferguson Senior divested himself of his business interests a few years before he died. Probably didn't trust Rolle to run them properly. He's been in and out of rehab. Cocaine addiction, one person told me. Alcoholism, another said. Severe personality disorder. Anger management problems."

"With all that going on inside him, he could be a viable suspect in Elwood's assault. So where is he now?"

"Your guess is as good as mine. I haven't been able to pin him down, but I'm working on it. The Atherton house isn't staffed right now, but I have the names and numbers of the housekeeper and maid who used to work there. It's not too likely I can track him down through one of them, but you never know till you try."

"Right. And keep trying to find out who Jersey is."

"I will." Mick added wryly, "As if I don't have anything else to do with my time."

5:41 p.m.

The printouts Mick had put on my desk contained the ugliest collection of data I'd ever read. Some of the groups I'd heard of before—Counter-Currents Publishing and the Loyal White Knights of the Ku Klux Klan—but there were also a few surprises.

The Society of Men; the Sisterhood; Women for Equality; Invalids and Others; Equalizers Anonymous. Simple names, sounding as if the groups were the do-good variety. But the profilers' summaries of their activities showed their true dark sides.

The members of the Society of Men were misogynists, devoted to smearing the reputations of women in positions of power—in either business or politics. The Sisterhood were the same, their targets male. Women for Equality didn't seek equality for the male gender. Invalids and Others seemed composed of individuals enraged enough to maim whole populations. The information on Equalizers Anonymous was jumbled and unclear, sounding like a rejected movie script.

The membership lists of some hate groups contained the names of people I had heard of, whom I never would have suspected of being bigoted. Worse were the names of individuals I knew or had thought I knew fairly well: a friend from college; a police officer whom I trusted; a neighbor of Rae and Ricky; a member of the board of supervisors; several people I'd read about in the newspapers; a neighbor of mine who was eighty years old and confined to a wheelchair. And then there were the anonymous others who were letting their rage run free.

Who or what was to blame for this?

The more I read, the more angry I felt—but it was an odd anger, infused with vulnerability. For the most part, I'd walked the streets of this city unafraid. And on those occasions when I had felt afraid, it was because of my profession, and I was usually armed against a known predator. Now the specter of hundreds of people who hated me for the color of my hair and skin, for my Shoshone features, haunted me. The thought that a blow to my head or a well-placed bullet could put me in the hospital—or worse—was unsettling.

Stop it, McCone. It's happened before.

Yes, it had. But racism hadn't been responsible that time.

I'd had to walk to Pier 24½, where we then had our offices, after my venerable MGB had run out of gas—faulty gauge, and I hadn't paid attention to it. It was July, the late night cold and misty, with few other people on the sidewalk; beyond the Golden Gate, foghorns moaned and bellowed. I let myself into the pier; it was silent, not even the tech companies that usually worked 24-7 showing lights. I climbed the stairs to our second-story loft, intending to retrieve the cell phone I'd mistakenly left on my desk when I'd gone out to dinner with Julia Rafael. Triple A was just a button push away.

But when I entered my office someone grabbed me, shoved me around. There was a flash of light and then a roar.

Gunshot. Close by.

Pain.

And then nothing.

I was extremely lucky the bullet hadn't killed me when it lodged in my brain. Many months of surgery, a long stay in the hospital and another in rehab, plus exhausting physical therapy had restored me to my former self. But still my level of awareness was raised every time I walked alone on dark streets.

7:17 p.m.

I tried to attend to routine business work, but kept coming back to the information on hate crimes. Finally I gave up and turned my full attention to what the Internet had to say.

A *Chronicle* reporter had divided local hate groups into five categories: White Nationalist; General Hate; Black Separatist; Anti-Muslim; Neo-Nazi. Their headquarters were scattered throughout the Bay Area, from San Francisco and Oakland to the supposedly quiet suburbs like Mountain View and Walnut Creek. Book clubs had been formed to read Nazi publications. One old man living in the Marina was responsible for most of the Ku Klux Klan's agenda in the city. No addresses, phone numbers, or website information for any of them was provided in the article.

The phone rang. The operative assigned to patrol the Marina district was checking in. So far tonight there'd been no sign of Jersey or the others I'd mentally started calling his gang of bar thugs. I'd been pretty sure they wouldn't return to the site of their assault on Elwood, but you never knew. I asked the op to keep patrolling until his relief came on.

8:49 p.m.

I'd been sitting for a long time looking out at the lights of the city, the Bay Bridge, the East Bay. A container ship moved slowly past Alcatraz toward the Golden Gate. I watched until it gained the open sea.

I tried to call Hy. Nothing, not even voice mail. What was the sense of having these handy phones when nobody was ever there to answer them? What was the point—?

Okay, stop that, McCone. No fretting tonight. Go home; the cats will be hungry.

Of course they were. Ravenous, in fact.

And so was I.

SATURDAY, DECEMBER 23

8:07 a.m

To my surprise almost everybody was at work, even on this Saturday before Christmas. We're a 24-7 operation, but there's no guarantee as to whom you'll find at the agency or what they'll be working on. A greater surprise was that Kendra was back at her desk, Jason Lieberman watching as she pointed out various items on her computer screen. I bypassed them and went directly to Mick's office to see if he'd come in early too.

He had. Still nothing on Jersey or Rolle Ferguson.

"You check the apartment building Rolle owns in lower Pacific Heights?"

"Nobody there at all. But I did turn up something that confirms that Rolle has racist tendencies. He was arrested for disrupting a Black Lives Matter rally in Oakland last summer. Was abusive to the police and almost everyone in the crowd, and it took three officers to subdue him. The case is still pending."

"So he went from picketing a high-school prom to a violent protest against blacks," I said, then asked rhetorically, "How the hell does that happen?"

Mick shrugged. "Why don't you ask Hy? He knows more about that kind of thing than I do."

After Hy's first wife had died, he'd set off on a reckless path of protesting antienvironmental causes. When I'd met him, but before we were a couple, I would often hear on the TV news that "Hy Ripinsky, premier agitator, has done it again." I'd rolled my eyes and watched him being hauled off to jail.

But then he'd mellowed—I liked to think because he knew I would've killed him had he gone on that way, but probably because he had the good sense to see what little progress he was making. Now he sat on the boards of various state and national ecological organizations. My crazy husband had turned into their voice of reason.

"Maybe I will," I said. "And you keep digging into Rolle's background, his circle of friends."

"Right. You thinking he could be involved with this Jersey and his crowd?"

"If he is a racist, it's possible. The bar owner, Willingham, described them as being well dressed and Jersey as wearing an expensive watch. A rich kid like Rolle Ferguson would fit right in with a pack like that."

Mick agreed. "Anything else on your mind?" he asked then.

"Yes—what's with Jason and Kendra?"

"Oh, he was having trouble with the flowcharts, so I asked her to come in and help him."

"Uh-huh."

"It's a serious matter, Shar. Might take weeks to resolve."

"I suppose we're paying well for her support."

"Yep."

"And extending all her employee benefits."

"Right."

"And at the end of this educational period, we'll keep Jason on as assistant to Kendra, whose salary will be increased because she will then be in a supervisory capacity."

Mick swiveled and gave me his faux-guilty look. "I only did what you would've done if you didn't have all this other stuff hanging over you."

"I know that, and I love you for it!" I jumped into his lap, put my arms around his neck, and pressed my cheek against his.

He held me for a moment, then pushed me off. "Jesus, Shar, the door's open. What'll people think?"

Those last three words resonated, and I burst into laughter. "You *are* your grandma's boy. Remember when she used to say that all the time? 'What will people think?'"

He stared at me, then started laughing too. Laughed until he almost fell out of his chair.

"God," he said between honks and snorts, "don't let me turn out like Grandma! I love her, but *please* don't let that happen!"

A smattering of applause came from the hallway: Julia, Ted, and Hy, who had been passing by when they'd heard the ruckus. They wanted to know what had caused it. We told them we'd go into it later, and I went back to my office.

12:37 p.m.

I needed a quiet break, so I went to Di Cassi's Italian Restaurant in Cow Hollow. My friend Chef D, as he called himself, installed me in an old-fashioned velvet-curtained booth and offered me a glass of what he called "the best Zinfandel in northern California." I don't have all that much of a palate for fine wine, but I had to admit it was splendid.

"What's your special for today?" I asked.

"Ah, my latest creation," Chef D said. "Fettuccini al Cubano. And you will be the first to taste it."

"I will?"

"In about five minutes."

"I can hardly wait. Tell me, Chef D, do rough and rowdy groups of young men ever come here?"

"Now and then, but my headwaiter is an excellent bouncer. Why do you ask?"

"Personal reasons. Does this group seem familiar?" I described Jersey and his gang. And I got lucky.

"Very familiar," Chef D said. He motioned for his headwaiter to come over. "Parker, what can you tell us about that disruptive bunch you waited on two days ago?"

Parker was short and medium brown, with the wide, pleasing features of a Filipino. He had served me many times before, and I recalled that he had a good memory.

He said, "They were the usual kind of young guys we get in here after they hit the clubs—well dressed, with more money than good sense. They'll probably be bankrupt before they're thirty. They were loud, drinking, but not enough to be removed from the premises. One of them made an ugly remark to me."

"What kind of ugly remark?" I asked.

"A comment on my heritage. He called me a Flip."

"Was the one who said that wearing an expensive watch?"

"Yes. A silver watch."

"Did any of the others call him by name?"

"Not that I remember."

"Were any names used? Rolle, for instance?"

"Rolle. An odd name. Yes, I did hear it used, but I'm not sure which one of them he was."

So now I had confirmation that Rolle Ferguson was mixed up with Jersey and the others. But whether they were the ones who'd attacked Elwood was still open to question.

"Anything else you can tell me?"

"Well, when they first came in I noticed one of them was limping."

"Badly?"

"Not very. It was like maybe he'd twisted his ankle or bruised his foot."

"Anything else?"

"He wore sunglasses. Seemed strange, that late at night."

Parker had nothing else to offer, so Chef D sent him away to the kitchen. He returned with a steaming plate, which he placed before me.

Chef D said proudly, "Fettuccini al Cubano."

I stared at pasta tangled with what looked like ham, peppers, red onion, Swiss cheese, and dill pickles. A slightly pink sauce was poured over it.

"Al Cubano," Chef D repeated. "Modeled on the sandwich."

"Looks good," I said in what I hoped was a cheerful tone.

"And naturally, it will cost you nothing," he added, smiling. "You are the first to taste it, as I said."

After the first bite, the human guinea pig found the dish delicious.

1:45 p.m.

The Divisidero Street condo Rolle Ferguson had inherited was one of four units in a two-story Edwardian, a single-family dwelling that had obviously been modified to accommodate two flats per floor. Its dark-brown paint was peeling and the outside staircase was littered with advertising circulars and envelopes of the sort junk mail comes in.

I parked in front and went up the stairs to the vestibule. Three of the four mailboxes beside the door had name cards in their slots, none of which read "Rolle Ferguson." The fourth slot had no card. I rang that bell. No answer. So then I tried the other three. No response from any of those either.

I did a quick canvass of the immediate neighbors. Two of the three who were home claimed not to know Rolle Ferguson or anything about him. The third, who lived across the street, did. She was a plump, cheerful woman whose expression soured somewhat when I spoke his name.

"I don't *know* him, not exactly, just know who he is," she said. "Him and his friends come and go. Why are you asking about him?"

"A personal matter. It sounds as though you don't much care for Mr. Ferguson."

"I don't. Noisy and rude, him and the others."

"When did you last see them?"

"It's been a while. Before Thanksgiving, anyway."

"Could they have been here on the nineteenth of this month?"

She thought about it. "Could've been. It was the day I took my granddaughter to see Santa, so—yes—maybe they were there on the nineteenth."

"How many were typically there besides Mr. Ferguson?"

"Four or five. I didn't bother to count."

"Do you know any of their names?"

"No, and I don't want to. Noisy and rude, like I said."

"Rude in what way?"

"One of them called me a nasty name because he didn't like the way I was looking at him. 'Keep your eyes to yourself, you blankety-blank kike.' Can you imagine? And I'm not even Jewish!"

3:05 p.m.

When I got back to the office, Ted told me that Mick had gotten a call a few minutes before and rushed out saying only that he was going home. Unusual for him, in the middle of the day. Mick loved the food trucks that frequented the area—offering anything from hot dogs to haute cuisine from all over the globe—as well as the sidewalk benches that afforded him a view of pretty, stylish women.

I went along the hall to the office Mick shared with Derek, hoping he'd told him why he was leaving.

"No, he didn't say anything," Derek told me. "Just busted out of here like a sheriff's posse was after him."

Oh Lord, Derek was still in his phase of fascination with old Western movies.

I was just sitting down at my desk when my cell buzzed. Mick, his voice unsteady. "I went home because one of my neighbors called with a nasty surprise. Come on over and see it."

3:39 p.m.

As soon as I drove up in front of Mick's house on Potrero Hill, I saw what it was that had upset him. The previously beautiful pale-blue façade and garage door had been graffitied in bright-red letters.

INJUN LOVER

GET OUT OF OUR TOWN

Now some despicable racist was taking out his or her quarrel with Indians on another member of my family! My blood pressure had risen, but at the same time I felt cold. I double-parked and ran up the stairs. The front door was open; I called Mick's name as I entered and he called back, "Kitchen." I noticed as I went there that the interior of the house had an empty look and feel now that Alison had moved her possessions out.

Mick sat slumped at the kitchen table, pouring into a glass from a bottle of Jameson Irish Whiskey. Coming home to that defacement must have been a serious shock. Mick's house, on the sunniest side of the hill, was a Victorian that he was restoring with the help of my older brother, John. The son of a multimillionaire—who had himself reaped a fortune in the tech boom—got almost as much pleasure out of hammering nails, drilling holes, and sanding floors as he did from exercising his considerable tech skills.

"Some mess, huh?" he said. "No way to scrub it all off."

"Your Uncle John can help you repaint." John owned a successful franchise, Mr. Paint. He'd learned his craft during long years as an apprentice. "I don't suppose any of your neighbors saw who did it?"

"None that I talked to."

"Did any of them bother to notify the police?"

"No, but I did. They're sending somebody over." He sighed, drank from his glass, and then said morosely, "I don't know why I even try."

"Try what?"

"To live a quiet, pleasant, normal life."

I went to the fridge and poured myself a glass of the Deer Hill chardonnay he kept there especially for me.

"Well, for one thing," I said, sitting down opposite him, "your life hasn't exactly been normal up to now."

He smiled faintly. "No, it hasn't."

Mick's father, Ricky Savage, had become a country music superstar, touring so much that his younger children sometimes failed to recognize him when he came home. His mother, my sister Charlene, tried to hold the family together, but it was hard to go it alone. They'd sent Mick north to Aunt Shar after a particularly disgraceful hacking episode involving the records of the Pacific Palisades board of education. Then his parents divorced and for a while chaos reigned. And what did Aunt Shar do? She turned Mick into a private investigator.

At the agency he teamed up with operative Derek Frye. In their spare time, they'd worked to build a real-time website, which had sold to Internet giant Omnivore for many millions. It wasn't exactly a rags-to-riches tale, since both came from money, but money wasn't what they were after; both were explorers, traveling into realms most of us never dream of. Their current project—very hush-hush—was something, Mick had told me, "that will set the tech world on its ear."

But in the meantime here he was, sad and beaten down and lost. After a long silence, he said, "It's just that when I was with Alison life had a feeling of normalcy."

Mick and Alison had been together for a few years, ever since he'd met her in the menswear department at Macy's, where both were looking for large socks. She was pleasant but quite reserved, and every so often I'd found her level stare unnerving, as if she were mentally psychoanalyzing its object.

Mick went on, "We'd get up late and rush around, kiss at the door. Come home, cook together, or go out. Watch TV or a movie or go to a club. Sure, I spent a lot of time on my computers, but for God's sake, that's my life's work."

I said, "I've known for a while why Derek's stayed with the agency—his promise to his father about working—but I've never asked you. Probably because I've been afraid of losing you."

He frowned. "I *like* the agency. It gives structure to my days, a little excitement when you send me out on an interesting case. And I like the people; we're almost a family, but without a black sheep. If I stayed alone, tinkering day after day in my studio, I'd end up like one of those old guys you see on the bad blocks south of Market, talking to myself and collaring people to tell them who I used to be."

"Well, we can't have that. Your grandma would throw a fit."

"How *is* she?"

I waggled my hand back and forth. "She and Saskia are

staying in one of the M&R hospitality suites, for security's sake. If you'd like, you could stay there too."

"Nope." He thrust his jaw out belligerently—he'd inherited that from Charlene. "I'm standing my ground. I still have the forty-five you gave me."

"That forty-five is a piece of shit. Besides, I doubt they'll come back."

"I almost wish they would."

"Mick…"

"Don't worry, I won't drink and I won't do anything crazy. I know how you feel about firearms."

"Well, recently I've reached a kind of middle-of-the-road opinion on the subject," I said. "Professionals who need a handgun on the job should undergo stringent background checks, rigid training, and frequent checkups. Responsible citizens should give a legitimate reason for having a handgun and also be meticulously backgrounded. Hunters—they're usually responsible, although you hear about all the accidents when they shoot each other rather than their prey. But anybody else—strictly no."

"They'll get hold of guns anyway."

I wasn't interested in engaging in a political debate. "I'd better let Sergeant Anders know about this latest outrage."

But when I called the Hall of Justice, she wasn't in. I left a message on her voice mail.

John arrived as I hung up. His gaze fixed on Mick and he went over and gave him a big hug. "'Taint all that bad, buddy. That's what relatives are for. Besides, I've been known to work cheap."

Mick stared into his drink. "I can afford your regular rates."

"Sure you can. But you realize I'm counting on you to support me in my old age."

Mick's lips twitched—a small smile. He said, "Only if you keep up with the housekeeping chores and don't insist on expensive vacations."

"Deal."

They shook hands, and then Mick put his head on the table and cried a little.

Time for me to leave.

4:59 p.m.

Hy wasn't there when I got home. I called his cell and got no response of any kind. That would have worried me if he hadn't come walking in just as I hit the Disconnect button.

"Thank God you're here." I said. "Every time I call your phone and don't even get voice mail, I tense up." Hy has a history of mysterious disappearances.

"My cell discharged. Shouldn't've. I think I need a new one."

"I'll get you one for Christmas."

Then I took a deep breath and told him about Mick's house being defaced. The news made him as angry as it had me. We sat down and discussed the implications. Had Mick been targeted because of the publicity about Elwood's attack? He'd been mentioned in some of the accounts as a relative. Or was it an indirect personal attack on me? Some sort of warped psychological game? And who was responsible? Jersey or Rolle Ferguson or another member of that bunch?

While we were speculating, Anders returned my call. No, she said, she had nothing to report. I explained what had happened and what I'd found out about Jersey and Rolle Ferguson. She was unfamiliar with the names, said she'd check on them.

She said, "My opinion is that it was directed at you, Ms. McCone, perhaps because of your Indian heritage. The perp wasn't able to find out your home address because you keep it carefully guarded. Is your nephew's listed?"

"Yes."

"So they targeted him instead. Despite what you told me before, the perp—or perps—may well be someone from your past. A former client with a grudge, or some other kind of enemy. I noted in your file that your house on Church Street was set on fire by Daniel Winters, a former client with a minor complaint against you."

I had a brief flashback to that night, the flames, the smoke. Choking as I tried to shoo the cats outside. Being felled by a flaming beam. Rolling on the fog-damp grass to put the embers out.

I shook off the memory and said, "It couldn't be Winters. He's in prison where he belongs."

"It could be someone with a similar grudge. What I'd like from you, Ms. McCone—a tall order, but I think it's necessary—is a professional biography. Major cases you've been involved in; cases where you've made enemies who are still at large; disgruntled former employees. Particularly any persons involved in the racist subculture."

God, how I hated to revisit those memories! I had already eliminated two possible suspects from our most recent major case, and it seemed unnecessary to me to go through all the many that had preceded that, because I still believed strangers I'd never encountered before were responsible. But all bases have to be covered, so I'd do as Anders asked.

I said, "You'll have it tomorrow."

9:11 p.m.

Hy went to bed early to read, and I sat on the sofa before a banked fire, legal pad in hand, to fulfill Priscilla Anders's request. I chewed on my number two pencil, something I hadn't done for years—probably not since junior high. But somehow it felt appropriate to regress, since I was delving into the past.

I went back through the highlights of my major cases as a private investigator, from the beginning.

First: The murder of an eccentric but well-liked antiques dealer. Now the murderer was serving a long prison sentence.

Second: A woman who lived in my building on Guerrero Street in the Mission had been killed. I'd been forced to shoot the perpetrator to save a friend whom he'd taken hostage.

A few years later: My friend and fellow investigator, whom I had nicknamed Wolf, and I each worked a case at— would you believe it?—a private investigators convention in San Diego. The perp was in prison, and no harm done—except I'd taken a bullet in the ass.

And then: Vietnamese refugees living in a shabby hotel in the Tenderloin. One of them was killed in the boiler room. After I'd apprehended the killer, I'd kept in touch with many of them—those who'd remained in the city, and those who'd fanned out to communities across the country.

A year later: A strange enclave in wealthy Pacific Heights called the Castles. Brick buildings, peaked slate roofs, and towering turret—all of it barricaded behind high walls. The family that had lived there were as odd as their surroundings. So far as I knew, some were still institutionalized, some had been released to society. I didn't keep in touch with any of them; lunacy is not my cup of tea.

So far I could identify no one involved in those early cases, not even those with good reason to hate me, who would have attacked me through my father. As far as I knew, none were racists.

I decided to take a break, got up, stretched, and went to the kitchen. I drank two glasses of ice water, stared at my own reflection in the dark windows, then returned to my list.

Bobby Foster: A young man had been convicted and sentenced to death in a "no body" case—one in which a comedienne had disappeared without a trace and, despite the lack of a corpse, the circumstantial evidence was overwhelming. The expression on his face when he'd first looked at me through the security glass at San Quentin had been so lost and despairing.

Hy on the shore at Tufa Lake. Environmentalists battling with a huge mining company threatening to reopen a gold mine in the hills—a move that would wreak havoc on the delicate ecosystem. We'd almost lost our lives in an explosion in that mine, set by the bomber, who had been blown up. Tufa Lake and the town of Vernon had been conflict-free since then…

I must have drifted off for a moment, but then more memories intruded: The explosion of the house belonging to my old college friend, T. J. "Suits" Gordon, attacked by the Diplo-bomber, as the press had dubbed him. The fatal, rigged plane crash of my former flight instructor, Matty Wildress, at an air show. My own crash on the volcanic ridge south of our ranch in the high desert. The return of Hy's evil former partner, Gage Renshaw, who was intent on destroying both of us, and the violent conclusion of his game…

Finally I gave it up, too tired to recall anything more, and went to join Hy in bed.

10:49 p.m.

But I couldn't sleep. None of the usual tricks I employ to induce sleep were working, and I knew they wouldn't, so I got up and went to the kitchen. My first thought was of Mick. He'd been drinking pretty heavily this past afternoon and talking about using his .45 if the racist taggers came back. I'd warned him to be careful, but with Mick you never knew.

I grabbed my phone and called his cell. He answered on the third ring, sounding hungover.

"Can any person you know ever get a good night's sleep?" he asked crossly. "What the hell do you need that can't wait till the morning?"

"I was worried about you."

"Worry away." A pause; it sounded as if he was gulping

water. "I spent a lot of the early evening hurling into the toilet, and a lot more talking with John. He just left."

"He have any words of wisdom?"

"Just that people leave you because they think they have to. Sometimes they come back and sometimes they don't. And that people who hate are going to hate regardless of what you do."

John should know about the former: he'd been left by a number of women for a number of reasons. But he soldiered on, ever hopeful…

"How are you feeling?" I asked Mick.

"How d'you think? Lousy enough to make me give up on both liquor and the female sex. But if you mean can I work, the answer is yes. The mind is a terrible thing."

"And work is a healing thing. I don't suppose you've done any more since yesterday?"

"No, but I put out a bunch of inquiries and by now I may be getting answers. Even in my addled state, I can read my e-mails. Wait a minute."

I knew he was padding into his computer room in the lonely, now-defaced Potrero Hill house. When Alison left, claiming that she didn't want to compete for his attention with a bunch of machines, he'd become more and more hooked into what I thought of as "the other world." At times like this, that seemed okay, but still I worried. There's so much personal estrangement in our society that sometimes I feel we're all wrapping ourselves in cocoons with our electronic devices. A doctor friend of mine says that touch is critical to a healthy life—and she doesn't mean contact through a plastic keyboard.

Mick came back on the line. "Nothing yet," he said,

sounding even grumpier. "I'll get back to you as soon as I have something to report. But don't expect anything soon."

"Why not?"

"It's the Saturday before Christmas, Shar. Other people have lives and holiday plans. What're you going to do today?"

"Visit the hospital again. After that, I don't know yet. Hang and rattle, maybe."

"Huh?"

"An old Western expression. I found it in one of Hy's books in his collection up at the ranch."

"God, your life sounds as gruesome as mine."

11:33 p.m.

The staff on Elwood's floor had gotten used to my odd pattern of visiting. They merely nodded at me as I passed through and started to enter his room.

Ma was there again by his bed, holding his hand and occasionally dabbing at her teary eyes with a handkerchief. He lay as still as ever, his breathing light, but his features seemed less waxen than before, his face more at rest. I watched from the doorway for a moment. You would have thought Ma was a grieving widow—except she'd never taken on this way when Pa or her second husband had died.

Fantasies, Patsy had said. How long had this been going on? Patsy claimed it had started when she—Patsy—was a little girl. Maybe earlier. But then why hadn't I noticed it? Why not John or Charlene? We'd been mostly out of the nest by then, but didn't absence from a person make their un-usual tendencies stand out? Or is it true that we see only what we want to see? Or don't see anything at all?

"Ma," I said, stepping into the room. Up close I could see her eyes were red and puffy.

"Sharon, thank you for coming. It's so difficult to see the poor dear man like this."

I went over and patted her shoulder. So bony and brittle it had become! "We'll have a celebration when he recovers."

She shook her head, returned her gaze to Elwood.

"Ma, would you mind if I had a few moments alone with him?"

"Why? Is there something you think you can do for him that I can't?"

"Of course not. It's just that…he's my father. I'd like to sit quietly with him for a bit."

Ma scowled and gave in with little grace. "I'll be in the waiting room."

When she'd left, I sat down and took Elwood's dry hand in mine. "Father," I said, "I wish you'd wake up and talk to me, help me find out who did this to you."

Did his fingers twitch, or was I imagining it?

"We're working very hard on finding out who the people are. I know it's not much satisfaction, but there's so much hatred in this world that even by punishing a few, it would be setting a good example."

A slight twitch, I was sure of it. But it could be he was having a nightmare.

"Oh, who am I kidding? Not you, Father, that's for sure." I closed and rubbed my eyes. "What I'm out for is revenge, plain and simple."

I sat like that for quite a while, then tucked his hand under the covers and left.

Revenge, plain and simple. Yes.

I didn't want to see Ma again just now—or suffer through another of her crying fits. I moved quietly down the hall toward the exit.

SUNDAY, DECEMBER 24

9:57 a.m.

I had just stopped in at the office when Saskia called my cell.

"I wonder if you would object to Robin and me going to your house this afternoon. I thought some of those old photographs I gave you may shed significance on what's happening now."

I didn't think so, but I said, "Sure. Robin has a key and knows the codes for the security systems. But I've got to warn you: the photos are sort of jumbled together in a file box. I haven't quite gotten around to sorting them and putting them in scrapbooks."

She laughed. "There'll be time for that when you're a very old lady. Where's the box?"

"Front hall coat closet. Is everything okay with the two of you?"

"Oh yes. The hospitality suite is nice, far better than most luxury hotels I've stayed in. And the food from downstairs is said to be divine."

"Well, good. Please use WeDriveU. Safer with them when

you go out." I recited the number that would bring a car around.

She asked, "Are all these security precautions necessary?"

"Just routine. Relax and enjoy being pampered."

"Yes, ma'am."

Something in Saskia's tone of voice told me she didn't believe a word I was saying. Didn't matter, so long as she was safe.

As soon as I ended the call, the phone buzzed again. Momentarily I thought that I'd like to get hold of whoever had invented cellular technology and throw them off M&R's roof garden. Sometimes it seemed as if all I ever did was talk to somebody or other on the phone.

This call was from Rob Lewis, the Identi-Kit man. He said Charley Willingham, the bartender from The Twenty-Second Century, had put off their meeting until late afternoon yesterday, which was why he hadn't been in touch sooner. When they finally sat down together, he'd compiled a few good Identi-Kit sketches.

"I'm on my way out to Christmas shop, so how about I drop them off at your office?"

"That'd be great."

10:55 a.m.

Lewis, someone I'd never dealt with in person, was a good-looking man, probably in his midthirties, with curly black hair and one of those little pointed chin beards that always make me think of caricatures of the devil. As he placed his portfolio on the table by the sofas, his eyes gleaming, I was again reminded of how enthusiastic he was about his work.

He contracted with city and county police agencies from all over northern California, as well as firms like ours. Private individuals too—people who were afraid their business associates or friends or newly discovered relatives weren't who they said they were; wives who thought they'd been whisked off to the altar under false pretenses.

In the old days, when the police had artists on call to produce renditions of suspects from witnesses' descriptions of them, the verisimilitude would vary according to the artist's skill and the reliability of the witnesses' powers of observation and memory. As demonstrated in criminology classes where professors stage an incident and then ask the students to describe it there are usually few descriptions that agree, in spite of the incident's having played out in close quarters.

Then came the Identi-Kits, with which technicians manually moved around various features—eyes, noses, mouths, chins, hair—to compose a likeness. Very time consuming and a strain on the witnesses' recollections. Now there was sophisticated computer software that had improved the process considerably.

Lewis flipped open his portfolio, took out one of the sketches. "This is of the man called Jersey," he said, "and it works best for Mr. Willingham."

The man in the sketch looked to be around thirty, with pale skin stretched over high cheekbones and a military-style haircut. His eyes were close set, the mouth turned down at the corners. "You can't tell from this, of course," Lewis said, "but the hair is blond."

He selected another. "This one also works for Mr. Willingham, but I don't know. It looks very much like a younger version of himself; could be he was influenced by his own image."

"Why would that be?"

"It happens for various reasons. In Willingham's case, he's frequently confronted by his image in the backbar mirror. Now this one"—he brought up a third sketch—"rings true to me. Nobody could imagine a face like this."

The subject had a narrow face pitted by acne scars; his eyes were small and mean, his thin lips twisted in what I assumed was a habitual sneer.

The last three sketches were fairly good likenesses of the other men, according to Willingham. One subject had dark-brown hair that the bar owner said he kept pushing off his forehead; he'd been the best dressed, in a dark suit and a red tie whose knot had been pulled loose. Another had been almost bald, casually dressed in chinos and highly polished loafers. The last was younger than the others, with fine blond hair and—as Mr. Willingham had described him—"a choirboy's face."

I asked, "Did Mr. Willingham remember anything more about any of them?"

"A few things. One, the bald guy, wore a lot of gold chains and bracelets; the guy with brown hair had a glittery stud in his right ear. The one called Jersey wore a fancy watch— maybe one of those iWatches."

"Yes, I know about that. Willingham mentioned it when I spoke to him."

"He told me he noticed because the guy kept checking it, as if they had someplace to be."

Yeah, out on the street assaulting innocent people.

12:25 p.m.

Rob Lewis had lifted my spirits. I thanked him and told him we'd be sure to use his services in the future. After he left, I went out to see if anyone else had come in. No. Mick was working at home, the others were out pursuing their real lives, and I was alone. I typed and printed a message to my staff, then left photocopies of the sketches on their desks, asking them to show them around in the Marina and lower Pacific Heights, where someone might recognize the people.

Now my spirits needed more lifting.

So what did I do?

I went shopping.

In spite of the fact that all our wrapped gifts had been steadily arriving by FedEx, I needed something to take my mind off business for a while and put me in touch with the season.

The holiday crowds around Union Square didn't bother me as they usually did. Last year they'd seemed pushy, greedy, and mean. This year I sensed a gentleness, as if they'd put the country's turmoil and anxiety on temporary hold. I actually smiled at some of the more frustrated-looking shoppers—and they smiled back. I contributed a few dollars to bell-ringing Santa Clauses. I bought a red carnation corsage from one of the street vendors, and he pinned it in my hair. Then I headed for Macy's.

Once inside the heady, perfumed atmosphere, holiday Muzak piped into my ears, I adopted the one-item-for-you, one-item-for-me approach.

This scarf is perfect for Patsy, and this other one is perfect for me. A red hat? I've never owned a red hat. Oh yeah, it looks just right.

I paused next to a counter full of beautiful ties. Hy hated ties; he wore them only for the occasional formal affair, and he owned plenty. Actually, all the males I knew were like him. Reluctantly I was about to move on, until I thought of Glenn Solomon: he'd been the first to extend the peace offering between us. This muted blue tie would be my token of forgiveness. And I'd spotted a stunning silk scarf at the counter where I'd bought Patsy's and mine that would perfectly suit Bette.

Driving gloves? The steering wheel on the Mercedes got awfully hot in sunny weather. Come to think of it, so did the one in Patsy's van. And Mick could use a new comforter—Alison had taken the good one. Hy and I had decided Rae and Ricky didn't need anything, but those candlesticks would look great on their dining table. Those sculpted red tapers too. And that fleece pullover—Rae loved fleece, wore it all the time. And Ricky could always use travel items. Toys for their new cat—whatever his name was.

My God, if I kept this up I'd max out my credit cards and be paying them off till next Christmas! Best to stop while ahead.

As I was stuffing my purchases into my car in Union Square's underground parking lot, I remembered the time years ago that I'd witnessed a fatal shooting here. The memory ended my frenzied focus on Christmas.

Money, a big bank account, plastic, and an ability to pay the bills after you run them up too high don't ensure happiness. Sometimes they bring the opposite. Of course, I didn't rush back to the stores and return the items. But the realization made me thoughtful as I headed home.

2:45 p.m.

The short drive from Union Square to Avila Street was tedious. In spite of local praise for the "new exceptional access" to the Golden Gate Bridge, cars clogged Van Ness Avenue and Lombard Street. I whipped a right turn, navigated stop signs on the side streets.

As soon as I turned onto Avila and saw the police cars and ambulance blocking the street, I knew something bad had happened at my house. Apprehension surged through me. Saskia, Robin…They'd been supposed to come here this afternoon for the box of photos…

I parked as close as I could get and jumped out. Ignoring a command from a uniformed patrolman, I pushed my way through the milling crowd.

A man in a dark jacket stepped in front of me. "Hey, you're Sharon McCone. Phil West of the *Chronicle*."

"Fuck the *Chronicle*! Get out of my way!"

Just then the front door opened and a pair of EMTs came out with someone strapped on a stretcher. Oh, God, no! I ran forward, straining to see. Black hair. Saskia? No, the outline of the body too slight.

It was Robin. Her eyes were closed and there was a smear of blood on her forehead, but there weren't any IVs attached to her. I reached her side before the EMTs could put her into the ambulance. A uniformed patrolman tried to get between me and the stretcher, but I said, "She's my sister!" and shoved past him.

Robin opened her eyes when she heard my voice. "Sharon. Don't worry, I'm okay…"

"Thank God. Saskia?"

"Her arm...but it's not broken. She's inside..."

I said to the EMTs, "Take good care of her." Then I rushed into the house. Saskia was in the entryway with Sergeant Priscilla Anders and another EMT, saying no, she didn't need medical treatment, she'd get to the hospital to see Robin under her own power.

"Ma'am," the EMT said, "I really think you should come along now."

"I said no and I meant it!"

God help the medical person or anyone else who tried to stand up to Saskia. She'd once even stared down late Supreme Court Justice Antonin Scalia. She turned to me as the cowed EMT left.

"Sharon, I was just about to call you. I'm so glad you're here."

"And I'm glad you and Robin are all right. What happened?"

"We came to retrieve the box of photos and there were two men here in the house."

Jesus! "What men? What did they look like?"

"I can't say. They were young, dressed all in black, wearing ski masks and gloves. They came at us and there was a bit of a...set-to. Then they ran out."

"How did they get in?"

"We don't know," Anders said. "There's no sign of forced entry."

"And I suppose nobody saw them leave."

"I have officers checking with your neighbors."

"Most of them work during the day. I'll be surprised if any of the ones who don't saw anything. People in this neighborhood mind their own business."

Saskia said, "There's something you need to see, Sharon. In the dining room."

The three of us went there. Mixed rage and horror welled in me when I saw what was spread over the only windowless wall. Part of the rage was directed at me. I shouldn't have allowed Saskia and Robin to come here unescorted, to be confronted by sick, dangerous bastards who would do something like this. Dammit, I should've been more careful!

What was on the wall was a painting of a dream catcher, one of those Indian wall hangings woven on willow hoops that resemble spiderwebs. Their powers are said to banish bad thoughts and dreams. Nowadays, the tribes consider them commercial assets and they sell like the proverbial hotcakes at tourist shops.

This one was anything but your traditional dream catcher. Entangled in its weblike interior and held on with staples were plastic replicas of dismembered body parts, bloody knives, weapons of all kinds. A cloth that I supposed was intended to resemble a blood-soaked shroud was pushpinned below the painting.

I could see signs of the "set-to," including black paint that had been spilled from a gallon can onto the floor. Angrily I kicked at the can; it rolled twice, leaking its contents, and then splashed more streaks of paint on the wall.

To Saskia's credit she didn't say anything like what my other mother would have: *Now you've made even a worse mess. That black paint is going to be impossible to get off the wall. You've got to learn to control your temper.*

Out of gratitude and relief, I turned and put my arms around her and snuffled, fighting back tears.

"I know," she said, "believe me, I know."

When I regained control I called Hy, but reached only his voice mail. I left a brief message describing what had happened here and asked him to come home ASAP.

Anders was still trying to figure how the intruders had gained entry.

She said, "This house is practically a fortress. It's equipped with nearly every surveillance and security device known to mankind."

"Well, Hy and I, because of our work, are high risk, so we accept the inconvenience."

"So how do you suppose they breached the systems?"

I said, "It couldn't have been through someone we know. We've never given out our security codes to anyone, except for trusted relatives like my nephew Mick."

"A highly skilled techie, then?"

"That's the only answer I can think of."

But I had a suspicion: Dean Abbot was an expert techie.

3:38 p.m.

Hy came home as soon as he received my message; he viewed the damage and was even more pissed off than I was. It was too extensive for a quick fix, and there was the possibility we'd be targeted again by the vandals, whoever they were. Anders was even more convinced now that the attacks were personally motivated, and my feelings tended that way. So did Hy's.

He said, "Let's go sit in the kitchen." I supposed he felt, as I did, that the dining room had been contaminated. Once we were there, he poured us glasses of wine and we sat at the table. Even the kitchen felt strange, violated. The cats felt the weirdness too; they were excessively clingy when they finally came around. Both of them must have hidden when the invaders came, and they'd stayed hidden until everybody else had gone.

"How in hell did whoever did this get our address?" I asked.

Hy shrugged. "With the Internet it's hard to conceal anything from smart hackers, no matter what you do. One of the bastards who broke in here or planned the break-in has to be a techie."

"I have one suspect: Dean Abbot, the guy who was hiding in our supply closet."

"Do you really think he's skilled enough to breach a state-of-the-art system?"

"Do you have any other suggestions?"

"Only a few, most of them employed at M&R."

"And the others?"

"There's a guy in Japan, but he's an old friend."

"What about that woman in Vienna?"

"Elisa? She died last year."

"Anybody in Silicon Valley?"

"Well, that's problematic. They're very protective of their talent. I'll call my buddy at TechWiz later."

"What's TechWiz?"

"Another start-up with promising prospects. Mick's hooked into that world. We should also have him contact the techies he trusts, ask if anybody knows who could've done this."

"He's already on it. I called and told him what happened before you got home."

We were silent for a time. Then Hy said, "I don't know, McCone. D'you feel comfortable hosting Christmas here in the house now?"

"No, and I'm not sure all the people we've invited for dinner would either."

"Well, I don't want to spend the holiday at the M&R building or in one of the safe houses."

"So who do we know who's a good cook and has a high-security residence?"

In unison we said, "Rae."

Rae was home when I called. I explained what had happened—she expressed her outrage in several four-letter words—and then asked if she and Ricky could accommodate us and our guests.

"Absolutely," she said. "The three younger kids're off to London visiting their mother and stepfather. It feels a little lonely around here."

"How's your security?"

"Not as tight right now as it should be. The alarm system's fine, but one of the patrol guards called in sick last night. Happens around the holidays."

Hy was on his phone to M&R, explaining the situation and instructing his operatives to conduct round-the-clock surveillance on our house. I motioned to him and said, "Ask them to beef up the security on Rae and Ricky's house too."

He nodded and made a thumbs-up gesture.

Rae said, "I'll still host dinner for the four of us tonight. And Christmas won't be any problem; I've been working on several dishes I planned to bring to your house anyway."

"What can I bring?"

"Yourselves and whatever you've bought for Christmas

dinner that won't keep." She added, "And bring the cats if you want to."

No way! "Uh, maybe," I lied.

"I know they hate the cage, but they might enjoy meeting our new cat."

"Oh, right—the new cat. What's his name?"

"Asshole."

"You're kidding!"

"Well, publicly we call him Jack, but he's officially named for most of the people in the recording industry."

3:57 p.m.

Saskia called as we were about to leave. Robin had been given a clean bill of health and was back at the M&R suite with her and Emi. I told her about the change of plans for Christmas dinner.

"What can we contribute?"

"Yourselves."

"No, seriously."

"Hmm. Can you get ingredients for fry bread here?" Indian fry bread, dipped in honey, is a treat I'd drive many miles for. And Saskia's was great.

"Flour is not exactly an exotic commodity. I also can find several kinds of honey."

"That's perfect."

"Happy to do it. We've also found an excellent wine shop around the corner."

"Wine will be welcome too."

"See you on Christmas, then."

4:30 p.m.

There had been no word from Anders, Mick, or the TechWiz people on their inquiries. As Mick had warned me, it was difficult to reach techies and ask favors of them at this time of year—or anybody else, for that matter. Like the majority of us, they were out doing last-minute shopping, standing in lines at grocery stores or in airline terminals, visiting relatives, or just cocooning until the hoopla—as Glenn called it—was over.

Hy and I loaded food and presents into my car. When he saw the number of my packages, his eyes widened.

"What the hell is all that?" he asked.

"Um," I said, "enough presents for the next decade?"

He laughed, came over, and hugged me. "I can't believe it, McCone. When did you go binge shopping?"

"Yesterday before I came home and found out we'd been invaded. If I hadn't, maybe I'd've gotten here sooner and prevented those bastards from doing what they did."

"Don't start blaming yourself. You couldn't have known."

We drove to Rae and Ricky's home in Sea Cliff, the exclusive enclave that stretches high on a bluff above the Pacific south of the Golden Gate. Neither of them was a status seeker, but the real estate agent who had shown them around the city was a commission seeker. She'd researched her clients well and quickly led them to a relatively private contemporary three-story house that descended the cliff toward a sand beach. It included room for a recording studio, six children of varying ages—who wouldn't live there all the time but would be frequent visitors—and a large cast of friends, musicians, and Zenith

Records executives. Also a workroom for Rae, the budding author; with the success of her handful of novels, the cast of visitors would soon expand to include other authors and publishers.

It was a happy outcome for two people who had suffered so much loss and deprivation in their early lives.

Before we reached the door, Mrs. Wellcome, Rae and Ricky's housekeeper, met us, properly uniformed and with a red rose in her hair. She set aside her reserve a bit and hugged both of us.

Rae and Ricky came out to greet us. She looked great in a blue velour lounging outfit that complemented her wide-set eyes and went beautifully with her red-gold curls. He was handsome as ever, sort of distinguished now that there were silvery strands in his thick chestnut hair. Rae had been my assistant at All Souls Legal Cooperative; she still helped me on difficult cases when she wasn't working on one of her novels. She'd started out to write what she called "shop-and-fuck" books, but instead her first novel turned out to be the critically acclaimed *Blue Lonesome*. Others had followed. Ricky had had an enormously successful career as a country singer and musician; he'd gone on to establish Zenith Records and produce some of the country's greatest performers.

Their relationship had begun when my sister Charlene, mother of their six children, had kicked him out of her life. I couldn't blame her; she'd put up with plenty during his philandering star days. But all that had changed now; Charlene was happily married to a new husband, Vic Christainsen, and with the advent of Rae, Ricky's philandering had stopped.

Rae said, "Mrs. Wellcome has just returned from two weeks in the Caribbean."

"Oh, which island?" I asked.

"Anguilla," the housekeeper said. "I didn't much like it. Too barren and touristy."

I agreed, but not for the same reasons; I'd been to Anguilla under harrowing circumstances.

"Well," I said, "it's hard to go anyplace these days that isn't touristy—especially at the holidays."

"Quite so." She nodded and excused herself to see about the appetizers.

When she'd disappeared into the kitchen, I whispered to Rae, "She go with one of her 'gentlemen friends'?"

"Undoubtedly. She packed some pretty racy underthings. Anyway, she's back, and—"

"No, it's too soon to ask her to deal with all the mess the holidays entail."

"She won't be the one dealing with it. I don't think I've told you, but Mrs. Wellcome has become an entrepreneur. She has a small stable of housekeepers working for her. I asked her to assign one of them to deal with it."

"Wonderful!"

"Yes, she is."

Mrs. Wellcome provided eggnog and snacks. The four of us sat near the pit fireplace in the living room, contemplating the Christmas tree.

"It's...kind of big," I said.

"It always is." Rae flashed a reproachful glance at Ricky.

He ignored it and looked fondly at the ten-foot-tall Douglas fir propped in the corner.

I said, "I think it's beautiful."

Rae: "Except for the two feet we had to chop off before we could get it into the house."

Hy: "That'll provide great kindling for fires."

A steely look from her.

He shrugged, grinning.

"Why," she asked Ricky, "do you always have to pick out something so enormous?"

"Why don't you like a big tree?"

"Well, my grandmother didn't celebrate Christmas. Said it was a waste of time and money."

"For me, big trees represent the Christmases I never had. When I was young, we were always too poor for a tree or much of anything else. Then, when Charlene and I were first married and we were starting our family, I was away on the road—Christmas gigs paid good. After I made it, there were all these other distractions. And then...I guess I just didn't care any more."

"And now?"

He put his hand on her knee. "Now I care very much."

Hy said, "Then it's time we stand this sucker up and decorate it."

6:10 p.m.

"Oof!"

"Get your foot off of mine!"

"Sorry."

"The tree stand's sliding."

"That's because the tree trunk's not in it."

"Do something!"

"Hey, it's in. Tighten those screws quick!"

"Ouch!"

"*What?*"

"Needles up my nose."

"Is it straight?"

"No."

"So which way is it tilting?"

"I can't tell. I'm *under* it."

"Asshole just ran up the trunk!"

"Which one?"

"Hah! The stupid cat!"

"Catch these lights and pull them around."

"I can't. They're snagged."

"On what?"

"A branch over there by you."

"Damn! Here they are. Grab them."

"Now they're tangled."

"How can they be tangled? We just took them out of their box."

"Give them to me."

"Now they're hopelessly snarled."

"I think more divorces result from putting on the tree lights than from adultery."

"That silver star was my favorite ornament when I was a kid."

"It's a wonder any of these survived."

"You guys gave us this little starfish the first year we were together."

"Hang that gold dove on a lower branch. When Asshole bites it—and you can guarantee he will—he won't do any damage."

"The ones in this box were my grandma's. Pot metal, but so pretty."

"What the hell's *that*?"

"A wooden cow with big pink udders that I found in a thrift shop."

"Here's a camel—he looks malformed."

"So does this bird—he's got no tail feathers, and the springs that're supposed to be his legs are giving out."

"What the hell—hang 'em all!"

9:24 p.m.

It had long been our custom to exchange gifts among the four of us on Christmas Eve, leaving the day itself for the kids and other family members. Bows and crumpled paper littered the floor. Jack (I refused to call him Asshole) had daintily climbed down the tree trunk, tiptoed around, sniffed everything, and then plowed through the discarded wrappings, digging tunnels and crawling into empty boxes. Now he had a big red bow stuck to his head, his tail was wrapped in green ribbon, and he'd gone to sleep under the tree.

Once we'd finished mauling the tree around and decorating it, it looked superior, filling up its entire corner of the living room. Somewhere Rae had cornered the market on authentic old-style lights with large bulbs, and the ornaments reflected their warm glow.

Briefly I thought of Cynthia Sharpe, the socialite in her Pacific Heights "mansion" with her professionally decorated tree. Her benefit for the Indian orphans who no doubt had been her second (or third or fourth) choice of charitable assignment couldn't possibly have been as pleasurable as our evening, but it had given me an idea. Next year Hy and I would host our own benefit for as many Indian orphans as we could fit into our house—only it would be for *them*, replete with toys, games, and goodies to eat, rather than the socialites Sharpe seemed to favor.

Mrs. Wellcome entered with more eggnog and a plate covered with just-baked chocolate chip cookies, and Rae urged her to join us. She did, staring nostalgically at the tree. "Reminds me...," she began and then broke off.

"Of what?" Ricky asked.

"Oh, of when my husband was alive. We used to yell and scream while we were putting on the lights, just like you people."

I was surprised to hear her speak of her past, as she seldom did.

"We didn't have any children to scandalize, though," she added.

"Neither do we, this year," Ricky replied.

None of the Little Savages, as I frequently called them, were present for this holiday, and the house felt empty. The younger children were probably having a great time in England, while his two older girls, Chris and Jamie, were off doing whatever young people of their age did.

Rae said to me, "I'm glad you gave me all your family's old ornaments before your house burned down."

"I knew you'd take care of them."

"Nobody else in the family wanted any?"

"Who? John's not into decorations; I'd planned to sneak over and hang a wreath on his door this year, but never got around to it. Ornaments are not the sort of item Charlene and Vic would be able to drag around on their global travels. And Patsy's an atheist and doesn't want to expose her children to 'such superstitious things.'"

"Kind of a bleak holiday season when all the other kids in school are celebrating it or Hanukkah."

"I think she cheats and celebrates anyway."

Mrs. Wellcome said, "I guess this is why we cling to this ritual: to remember the happy times in the past and hope for more in the future."

We were contemplating her remark when my phone buzzed.

I'd put it into my pants pocket and forgotten all about it. I pulled it out, stared at the caller's number on the screen. SF General. When I answered, my voice was curiously unlike my own.

It was a head nurse in ICU, and I couldn't have asked for better news.

Elwood had regained consciousness.

11:51 p.m.

Hy and I rushed to the hospital. Elwood was lucid and able to speak, the charge nurse told us, but we must be careful not to tire him. "Five minutes," she said, tapping her watch.

My father looked surprisingly good. No more waxiness to

his features, no more twitching muscles. "Daughter," he said haltingly, "so sorry I spoiled your Christmas."

"Spoiled it? You've just given me the best present I've ever received."

He smiled faintly as I took his hand.

"How are you feeling?" I asked.

"Weak."

"That's understandable. Are they giving you enough pain medication?"

"Too many."

I knew about my father's aversion to painkillers, so I said, "I'll speak to Dr. Stiles about that."

Hy asked, "What do you remember about the attack, Elwood?"

Slight headshake. "Very little...I was looking in the jewelry store window when men appeared...called me foul names, and beat me."

"How many men?"

"Three, four, five..."

"Did you get a clear look at any of them?

"Can't remember."

"That's perfectly natural, after a traumatic experience," I said. It had been some time until I recalled the moments before the bullet entered my brain. Now I did, all too often, and I wished I couldn't.

Elwood felt the same. "Maybe not remembering is a blessing," he said.

"Not necessarily," Hy said. "If your memory returns, you might be able to recall something that will help us catch the assailants."

"You...have no idea who they are?"

We were not about to tell him of Jersey and his gang, or the racist attacks on Mick's house and on ours, or the close calls Saskia and Robin had had. It would've been cruel to burden him with all that in his condition. "Not yet, Father. But we have a few leads—"

Elwood sighed. "Please...the truth. Can you...ever find them?"

"Yes, I can. And soon. I promise you that."

He seemed about to say something else. But then he sighed and his eyes closed.

His nurse, who had apparently been watching at the door, came in and said, "You'll have to leave now. Mr. Farmer needs his rest."

When Hy and I stepped out into the foggy San Francisco night, he said, "We'll check in with Rae and Ricky and then go home. And maybe get a good night's sleep for a change."

"I hope so."

"We will. The box of chocolates that I put on the kitchen table before we left is the perfect remedy for sleeplessness."

MONDAY, DECEMBER 25

Elwood's being out of danger had given me hope for today. And when Mick called, I felt even more cheered by the news he had for me.

"Derek finally got a lead on the guy called Jersey," he said. "It took this long because we figured it was a nickname, spelled like the state. Wrong. It's a Polish name spelled j-e-r-z-y. Jerzy Capp. A dubious character."

I was still in bed, a second cup of coffee in hand. I sat up straighter, put the cup on the nightstand. "What're these 'dubious' things he's done?"

"The usual—not quite getting caught for shoplifting, kiting checks, and various scams that didn't net him much. Stealing cars off lots and claiming he was just taking them out for test drives. The usual small-time cons. And there's another definite connection between him and Rolle Ferguson."

"The racist kind?"

"Yep. Jerzy got into the white supremacist crap in prison, and he and Ferguson are reputed to be tight. Word is that he's been living with Rolle on and off since they met at an anti-immigrant rally a year ago."

"Were you able to get a current location on them?"

"Not yet, but if I get lucky I may have something by tonight."

I heard the front door open. Hy, back from whatever errand he'd gone out to run.

"Mick," I said, "you do know what day this is?"

He made a huffing noise; he wasn't expecting the holiday to be pleasant. "Yeah, sure I know."

"Do you intend to sit home working on Christmas? I thought you were going to dinner at Rae and Ricky's."

"I don't really feel like socializing. Working keeps me from thinking about Alison."

"Why don't you call her?"

"No, she's made it clear—I'm out of her life."

I didn't try to contradict his statement because I don't believe in Christmas miracles any more than Mick does.

"Okay," I said, "have it your way. But please join the rest of us for Christmas dinner."

"Maybe, if I feel up to it," he said, and broke the connection.

God, I hurt for him...

Hy came upstairs, peered through the door. He had a large tote bag in his hand. "You look kind of glum."

"Mick." I gestured futilely. "He's hiding in his work."

"Well, he has a right to after what's happened to him lately."

"Still, it's not healthy for him to be alone on Christmas."

"Did you call or did he?"

"He did, with news that may be important." I related

what Mick had found out about Rolle Ferguson and Jerzy Capp. "Sure seems like they could be the bastards who assaulted Elwood and keep giving the rest of us so much grief."

"Yeah, it does. Mick said Jerzy's living off of Rolle?"

"Yes."

"I wonder which one is dominant."

"Probably Rolle. He's the one with the money and the smarts, so it's likely he's calling the shots."

"In any case we need to know more about these guys, McCone."

"Mick said he might have some info on their whereabouts by tonight."

"Let's hope so."

He sighed and sat down beside me, setting the bag between us. Some of the contents rattled.

"What've you got in there?" I asked.

He pulled out a ball festooned with red and green ribbons and held it above my head.

"Mistletoe!" I said.

"Yup." He leaned over and kissed me.

"You went out early for *mistletoe*?"

"And a few other things. Champagne. That pâté you like. Brie. Sourdough. And, for dessert, raspberry tarts from what's-his-name's restaurant."

"Chef D's."

"Right."

"And this is Christmas lunch?"

"You betcha. We've got to eat, and we're not due at Rae and Ricky's till three."

2:33 p.m.

We were getting ready to leave for Rae and Ricky's when the landline rang. Thinking it might be Mick, I picked up.

A rough, distorted man's voice said, "The only good Indian is a dead Indian." And then he broke the connection.

I replaced the receiver, angry and a little shaken. The bastards had invaded my home again, this time on Christmas day.

Hy came to the archway from the dining room. "What?" he said.

"Nuisance call." I must have looked as disturbed as I felt; he put his arm around my shoulders, hugged me tight.

"McCone," he said then, "go upstairs and get duded up in that killer blue velvet shirt I gave you."

"Why? I was planning on wearing it New Year's Eve."

"Wear it today—just don't slop gravy on it." He gave me a little nudge toward the stairs.

3:10 p.m.

Briefly we stopped by the hospital to wish Elwood a good evening, but he was asleep and the nurse urged us not to wake him. "He's had a decent day," she told me, "and his vitals are stable. We're hopeful of more improvement as time passes."

"Has he recalled anything about the attack?"

"Ms. McCone, I know you're anxious to find out who the

men who did this to him are, and he is too. But our main goal is his successful healing, and that means rest."

"I know."

God, how I do know that—from deeply personal experience.

5:15 p.m.

Rae's turkey-and-all-the-trimmings dinner was perfect: a golden-brown bird; her special dressing with chestnuts, apples, sausage, and dried apricots; creamed onions; cheese-and-potato casserole; cranberry sauce; and an exotic mixed green salad.

Everybody stuffed themselves: Saskia (whose arm injury had required no more than two stitches and a bandage); Robin and Emi; Hank, founder of All Souls Legal Cooperative and my best friend since college; his wife Anne-Marie, another attorney; and their daughter Habiba. Ted and his partner Neal. Derek. Even Mick, who had decided to join us after all; his lonely, violated house had been too much for him to bear on Christmas. The only one at the table who had just picked at her food was Ma. She was strangely subdued about Elwood's having regained consciousness—maybe because she was afraid he would disrupt her fantasy about the two of them. She, Saskia, Emi, and Robin left shortly after dinner. I could tell Robin wished she could stay longer, and resolved to invite her over more often.

After they left, the rest of us exchanged yet more gifts. Nothing expensive, mainly local crafts and artisan wine, beer, and foodstuffs that we'd picked up at the holiday fairs. Jack the cat jumped through the wrappings as he had the night before and then curled up in a big terra-cotta pot that held an overgrown ficus plant. The rest of us lounged around the living room, and occasionally someone or other would yawn.

Anne-Marie and Hank looked half-asleep. Habiba was passed out on Hank's lap. Ted and Neal were curled up at opposite ends of the couch, their feet touching. Neal was snoring.

Ricky went to the kitchen to open more wine.

The Savages' landline rang. Rae picked up warily, listened, and said, "Great news!" and gave the receiver to me. Patsy, at home in Napa with her children and Ben, her current lover. "Guess what?" she said. "Ben and I are engaged!"

"To be married?"

"What else does *engaged* mean? He even gave me a ring."

"So when is the big event happening?"

"As soon as we can get permission from the kids."

"What!"

"This will have a big impact on them. They deserve to have a say in it."

Modern parenting! We talked a little bit more, I asked for Ben and congratulated him and then went back to share the news.

A few minutes later, the door chimes sounded. Rae went to see who it was. When she came back she said, "One of the new M&R security guards."

"Some sort of problem?"

"No. Just checking in to let us know everything's all right. Frankly, it's a pain in the ass having them around all the time. I'm beginning to feel as if I were living in a fortress."

"Me too. They're all over Avila Street."

She nodded and fell silent. I suspected she was thinking of the security on Ricky's tour when she was first with him—and how badly it had malfunctioned because nobody on his staff suspected that the stalker they were supposed to be protecting him from was someone with easy access to him. If it weren't for Rae's detecting skills, things could have turned out badly for all concerned.

To distract her I said, "I guess we should do something about this mess, so Mrs. Wellcome's employees won't quit on her."

11:33 p.m.

As tired as Hy and I were when we got home, we had a glass of wine and reflected on the day and Elwood's recovery. I loved my gift from my father: somehow Rae had divined why Elwood had been outside the jewelry store where he was attacked, and had bought the aquamarine earrings as a gift from him to me. The same with Hy's new aviator watch. Rae had supplied catnip for the beasts who, happy to have us home, snuffed it up and then rocketed around the house like lunatics.

"This has been a pretty good Christmas," I said, "considering how the season started."

"Better than 'pretty good,' now that Elwood's back with us."

"Tomorrow, though, we've got to get up to speed and nail the bastards who attacked him."

"We will."

"Really? I don't know. I keep waiting for the other shoe to drop."

"Stop waiting, have one of those chocolates, and come to bed. Shoes won't rain until tomorrow."

TUESDAY, DECEMBER 26

5:45 a.m.

In the middle of the night, though, we thought the other shoe might have dropped.

A ponderous knocking sounded at the front door.

Hy's hand went to the bedside drawer, came out with his .45. "Stay here," he said.

"No way." I grabbed my bathrobe from a nearby chair.

The knocking was repeated. As we went down the stairs, I couldn't help but remember the last time we'd been summoned out of bed by visitors in the middle of the night. The police again with more bad news?

There was a judas window in the door. Hy peered through it, then eased it shut.

"Who?" I whispered.

"Some freakish-looking guy."

"Let me see."

The figure outside had a ski cap pulled down over his brow and a heavy beard, and he wore a denim jacket and a red bandanna around his neck. When he lifted his head and knocked again, I had a clearer look at his high, beetle-browed forehead. Recognition made me let out the breath I'd been holding in a relieved sigh.

I said, "It's Will Camphouse, my symbolic cousin from Tucson."

Hy relaxed too, and tucked the .45 into the pocket of his robe as I unlocked the door. Will came inside, hugged me, then pulled off his ski cap and shook out his black hair. I introduced him to Hy and then took his jacket and cap.

"What is this?" I asked. "A disguise?"

"The cap I bought in the hospital gift shop when I saw the fog was coming in—more rain than fog now. The beard is on account of a bet with a friend who claimed that Indians can't grow them thick. He's out fifty bucks. And, besides, I kind of like it."

"Me too."

"I went straight to the hospital to see Elwood, but they wouldn't allow it. The night nurse told me he regained consciousness last night and his condition is good."

"He's getting stronger every day. Still can't remember anything about the attack, though."

"Where are Saskia and your other mother?"

I explained about the M&R hospitality suite.

"I'm glad they're safe."

Hy fetched the bottle of Zin we'd opened earlier and three glasses. After he'd served us, Will took a sip and smiled in appreciation. "Here's to the death of another bit of erroneous popular wisdom about Indians: that one whiff of alcohol makes us all turn into slavering drunks."

We toasted and drank.

"I went up to Montana to make sure Elwood's cabin and studio were secure and to make sure his friends on the rez stayed put. They all did except Emi, who had already left to come here. I did have a great Christmas dinner at the community center. Everybody sent their best wishes to Elwood."

"He's a popular man on the reserve."

"And not so popular here in the city."

"The police think the attack on him was motivated by somebody with a grudge against either Hy or me, and I'm coming around to their viewpoint. I thought it was a random hate crime to start with, then escalated into something more when the perps found out he's my father. I'm still not sure, but there's a lot of hate in our city—against Indians, blacks, Jews, Hispanics, Chinese, Japanese, LGBT people, and any other minority you can think of."

"Not so different from Tucson, although the Hispanics take most of the heat there. And it's on a much smaller scale."

Hy finished his wine and stifled a yawn.

I asked Will, "So what're your plans now?"

"I've got a leave from the agency. I guess I'll hang around and see what happens with Elwood. Maybe I could help you investigate."

I remembered the times my brother John had "helped" on my investigations. Could Will be as much of a distraction as John had been? I doubted it, but I had no intention of finding out.

"Well," I said, "let's talk about that in the morning. You look really beat."

"I am. I had to go through Denver and then take a couple of feeder flights and then rent a car to get to the rez. Coming back here...Who says that air travel has revolutionized the world? What I'm gonna do is drive over to Lombard Street and crash in the first motel I see that doesn't look like it's got bedbugs."

"No, you're not. You'll stay here. And I promise: no bedbugs."

9:31 a.m.

Early in the morning Mick had e-mailed color photographs he'd accessed of Jerzy Capp and Rolle Ferguson. Jerzy's matched Rob Lewis's sketch of a thin-faced man with high cheekbones, but when the photo was taken his sandy hair had been long and he'd worn a wispy beard. His eyes were a luminous blue. Rolle was short, dark complexioned and clean shaven, his eyes hooded so their color wasn't apparent. Something about the two men's stances—both photos were full-body shots—struck me as menacing.

When I called Mick to thank him, he said, "Some pair, huh? All-American white racists you wouldn't want to meet in the proverbial dark alley."

"No further information on their whereabouts?"

"Nope. I made contact this morning with the former housekeeper at the Atherton place. She said Rolle fired her and the other help in October. She has no idea where he is now. Could be the summer home in Tahoe—"

"The operatives in our office in Reno can take care of that. As for Europe—no winter vacation for you."

He gave a martyred sigh. "My work is never done, et cetera, et cetera," he muttered before he hung up.

10:13 a.m.

I was drinking coffee in the kitchen when Will came loping down the stairs, a spring in his step showing that he was well rested. I poured him a cup and motioned him to a chair at the table.

"Breakfast?" I asked.

"Never eat it. What can I do to help on this investigation?"

"I think my staff can handle it, but thanks anyway." I asked, "So what're your plans for the day?"

"I've got some personal business to attend to. And then I'll drop in on Elwood."

I said, "I doubt I'll have time to drop in at the hospital, but we'll touch base later."

1:48 p.m.

Nothing was going on at the office. I'd saved a bunch of brownies from yesterday's dinner—Rae always bakes too many—so I distributed them to our skeleton staff.

A few minutes later, my weekly rose arrived. Years before, when I'd scarcely known him, Hy had begun the practice of sending me a single long-stemmed rose on Tuesdays. The first ones had been yellow—my favorite—but as our relationship had deepened, the colors had also deepened, finally reaching a red so dark that it was nearly black. This red had supplanted yellow as my preference. I added it and water to the bud vase I keep on my desk and fingered its soft petals. Hy and I didn't believe in traditions—we'd stopped giving each other Valentine's cards because for three years we'd exchanged the same ones. But the roses persisted, and every time I received one I was thrilled.

Hy was waiting in his office for me and suggested lunch, but then he had a call from a woman named Terry Neditch at TechWiz, the firm he'd contacted about savvy people in the Bay Area. He put his phone on speaker so I could listen and join in the conversation. "I have information for you: an off-the-charts techie, Dean Abbot. If anyone could pull off the kind of scam you people have been subjected to, it's him."

Dean-of-the-closet.

Hy said, "This Abbot—exactly who is he? What's his background?"

"Grew up in Los Altos. Attended Stanford but dropped out in his sophomore year. Founded a start-up four years ago called EStuff—it sold castoffs that other sites and stores couldn't move. It went under two years later. Since then his name appears here and there, but nobody knows exactly what he's doing."

"This EStuff sounds like a winner. Why did it fail?"

"Inattention on the part of Abbot. Apparently he's one of these guys who leap around from one project to another and never settle into a leader's role. He's been involved in other start-ups, but most of them went under after his departure."

I said, "A dabbler, then. A follower."

"I guess to him the becoming is more interesting than the being."

"Does your information tell you if Abbot has ties to the white supremacist community?"

"I was just about to get into that. He's connected. Has an unpleasant blog under an alias, Michael Bonds, regularly posts inflammatory opinions. But unlike Ferguson and Capp—whose names he's mentioned on his blog—the alias tells me he keeps a low profile. No protest rallies, passing out flyers, that kind of stuff. I can't speculate as to why, but he doesn't seem to want public scrutiny."

"You have an address for him?"

"Yeah, in Piedmont." She read it off to us.

Piedmont. A small, semiaffluent residential community in the Oakland Hills.

When we ended our call with Neditch, Hy asked me, "This Abbot—why d'you suppose he's intent on keeping such a low profile? Most of those hard-core activists thrive on publicity."

"Well, when you're low profile, you can get away with a hell of a lot more."

"Such as what? Assaults on innocent citizens?"

"Could be. His low-profile attempt isn't working all that well, anyway. Publicizing his opinions—even under an alias—on the Net where the world can see them, how stupid is that?"

"So he's stupid or confused or even psychotic."

"Wonderful choices," I said. "You want to come along to Piedmont with me?"

He did, but as luck would have it, he couldn't. He received another call just as we were getting ready to leave, and when he answered and listened for a moment, he mouthed the words, "My contact at the Bureau," to me.

Then: "So what's the situation there? The hostage? Yeah, I know him. What happened? Jesus! Don't these clients pick up on what we try to teach them? Send me the whole pdf on my cellular and a chopper...No, I'll go straight from SFO to Orly. Let me know who's going to meet me there."

My stomach wrenched. I was used to Hy's being summoned away at odd times, but given what was going on here, this was a particularly bad time.

"Sorry, McCone," he said when the conversation ended. "Hostage situation brewing in France—Syrians involved. I've got to get going."

"Can I drive you—?"

"No, they're sending a chopper to take me to the airport." He was already dragging out the travel case he kept in his office closet, checking to see if he had his passport and various other government papers.

I asked, "The chopper's coming here?"

"Yep."

"I'll go up to the roof with you."

He dropped the bag, pulled me close, and tipped my face up to his. "No, McCone. The last thing I want to see today is you growing smaller and smaller on that roof."

He kissed me, then said, "I'll call you," and headed up the stairs. It wasn't long before I heard the chopper's noisy blades churning the air above the building.

I dropped heavily down into my desk chair, wondering how long it would be before his customary promise, "I'll call you," would irrevocably be broken. Or how long before his customary warning to me—"You be careful out there"— would no longer be relevant.

Enough torturing myself. Time to get back to work.

I slipped my .38 into my purse for insurance before I left

the office. I was in a spooky mood and if you have a carry permit these days, it's always a good idea to protect yourself. There are too damn many unstable people out there packing loaded weapons that they shouldn't have.

2:02 p.m.

The address Neditch had supplied for Dean Abbot was a small house on a hilltop that overlooked a good portion of the East Bay. White stucco with the obligatory red-tiled roof. Nothing outstanding about it, except that it was large and surrounded by a lot of land. I rang the bell; chimes sounded within. No answer. I rang again.

And the door was opened by a human egg.

The short man who stood before me had a perfectly ovoid shape. Even his hairless head, short arms, stubby legs, and small feet contributed to the Humpty Dumpty illusion.

If he was surprised to see me, he managed to mask it. "Yes?" he said impatiently.

"Dean Abbot, right?"

"Yes. Who are you and what do you want?"

"You know who I am. You were hiding in a supply closet at my offices on the twenty-first and scared the hell out of one of my employees."

He wasn't at all embarrassed. "Oh, right. One of your people told me I was no longer welcome on the premises—just as you're not welcome here."

"Just why *were* you on the premises?"

His gaze shifted. "Uh, doing a favor for a friend."

"What friend?"

No reply. Then, "A friend who's interested in information on the high-tech security industry."

"And you thought you could gather some in the *supply closet*?"

"It was a start. Now if you don't mind…"

"I do mind. I'm not ready to leave yet, not until we talk about the racist attack against my father."

The attempt to catch him off guard failed. "Why come to me? I don't know anything about it."

"Your name's been linked to two men—Rolle Ferguson and Jerzy Capp—who may have been involved."

Still no reaction, other than a cold stare. He said in a snotty tone, "I don't believe that. I've never heard of either."

"Sure you have, Mr. Abbot. You've mentioned both on your blog."

"What blog?"

"I should have said Michael Bonds's blog."

"Michael mentions a lot of people on his blog. Most of them I don't know personally."

"So Michael Bonds is who? Your alter ego?"

"Something like that."

"Isn't that dishonest?"

"People can say anything they want or be anybody they want on the Internet."

"That's true—until what they say catches up with them."

"What's that supposed to mean?"

"I think you know. I got your name from a company called TechWiz. They say you're one of the best hackers in the state."

"I am *not* a hacker. But they're right about me being the best at what I do."

"And just what is that?"

"I'm a researcher. I can find out anything about anybody."

"Including me."

"Anybody. Nobody has better computer skills than I do."

"Could you breach a highly sophisticated home alarm system?"

His gaze shifted, turned wary. "What kind of question is that?"

"One I want an answer to. The system on my home was breached recently."

"And you think *I* did it? You're crazy, lady. I'd never do anything like that. It's illegal."

"So is hacking into private files."

"I told you, I'm not a hacker—"

"Where were you last Saturday afternoon?"

"Christmas shopping, not that it's any of your business."

"Where?"

"Right here in Piedmont."

"Can you prove it?"

"Damn right I can, not that I have to. Quentin!" he called out over his shoulder.

Footsteps sounded behind him. A second egg, taller and not quite as round, peered over his shoulder. My God, a matched set.

Abbot said to me, "This is Quentin Zane, my roommate. Quent, tell this…person where I was and what I was doing on Saturday afternoon."

"Christmas shopping with me. Why?"

"Satisfied, Ms. McCone?"

No, I wasn't. It was a prearranged alibi if I'd ever heard one.

"What's all this about, Dean?" Quentin Zane asked petulantly.

"Nothing either of us needs to be concerned about." Then, to me, "I have nothing more to say to you, Ms. McCone, now or ever." And he shut the door in my face.

3:16 p.m.

As I walked back to my car I thought about Abbot's being involved with Jerzy and Rolle and whoever their cohorts were. It worked for me. Also I had little doubt that Abbot was the one who had orchestrated the break-in at my home. The problem was in proving it. That was always the primary difficulty in dealing with technology: it was too amorphous. Individuals' movements were too hard to trace, and anybody who had the skills to trick the system could put anything over on you.

What about Quentin Zane? Was he involved in some way with that bunch too? In my car I called Derek at the office— Mick already had too much on his plate—and asked him for background checks on both Abbot and Zane.

I sat slumped in the car for a time, my head tilted back. *When did things get so damn complicated?* I wondered. Then, after a few moments, I thought, *Well, maybe they haven't.*

When you got right down to it, people were much the same as they'd always been—their motivations, emotions, hopes, and dreams. Didn't matter that they went about achieving them with new technologies, more speed, and more ease. The underlying desires were still there; they were what I should be tapping into.

But how to do that?
Take a long drive and think about it.

4:00 p.m.

Traffic was light during this post-Christmas week when many took time off work to travel or enjoy staycations. I coasted through the Bay Bridge Toll Plaza, made good time across the city, and was soon on Interstate 280 heading south.

As I was passing the shopping mecca at Serramonte—Walmart, Toys "R" Us, Kmart, Home Depot, and dozens of their ilk—I received a call from Derek. He had no further information on Dean Abbot, but Quentin Zane, he said, was another computer nerd like his roommate; he had a good job with one of the software companies that had recently moved from Silicon Valley to San Francisco, and no apparent ties to white supremacists. So maybe he knew what his friend Dean was into, and maybe he didn't.

My drive took me all the way to San Jose, a tangle of freeways surrounded by high-rise office buildings and smaller manufacturing firms. It was once a sleepy town in the orange groves, but its population has swelled to over one million, making it the third most populous city in California and the tenth most populous in the United States. With such unchecked growth have come problems—smog, mainly. Today it was strong enough to clog my nostrils and make my eyes burn, so I got off at a downtown exit and drove back up the Peninsula.

Several miles later I noticed the Trousdale Avenue exit

off 280. On impulse I took it and then turned onto Hillway Drive. The weather was warm down here and I lowered my window. The familiar scent of dried grasses, pine, and oak leaves rushed in at me; although it was late in the year, the persistent drought of the past few years had increased the fire danger in these hills. They were still attractive despite the number of dead and dying trees, and the fragrant air brought memories of lazy summer days.

I used to come here with a man—briefly my lover—who'd been a professor at nearby Stanford University. We'd spread our picnic blanket on the shore of man-made Searsville Lake and try to conjure up the ghosts of the small but thriving town that had been inundated in the late 1890s by the damming of a creek to create alternative sources of water. Some people claim you can still see shadowy images of the town in the water, but I never have.

On other days we'd have our lunch near Frenchman's Tower, a medieval-looking, silo-like structure containing a water tank and a library, erected in the 1870s by an eccentric Frenchman who used many aliases and refused to divulge his true identity—another of the Peninsula's mysteries. He returned to France finally, after selling the tower to Leland Stanford, and it has stood ever since.

As I passed the turnoffs that would take me to my former haunts, a sharp wind began to blow; it would bring in fog from the coast later. Now it whispered in the trees and carried the additional scents of turmeric and bay laurel. A white-tailed deer flashed across the road ahead, startling me. I saw no houses, but tall iron gates and the occasional peak of a roof indicated they were there.

Atherton is one of the wealthiest communities in America, with an average per-household income approaching a million dollars. Homes go for much more, the average being upwards of six million. Long ago the citizens—all of them influential—opted to preserve the residential, rural feel of their open space, and by and large they've succeeded. I'd worked another case in this vicinity, and the tree-lined lanes that concealed mansions had struck me as somewhat sterile in spite of their beauty.

I was now passing the notorious Wellands, a ninety-two-room manse built in the early nineteen hundreds by one of the heirs to a mother lode fortune. It has a strange history: many owners, all of whom only sporadically lived in it; two teenaged girls who had been raped, beaten, and left for dead on the grounds in 1989 by a vagrant posing as a security guard who lured them onto the premises with the promise of a tour. Some people who lived in the area spoke of the estate in low voices, as if afraid of awakening the ghosts who were said to inhabit it.

I hoped the Ferguson estate—Bellefleur, Mick's file had said it was called—contained no such entities, dead or alive.

Probably it contained no one, period. I hadn't been able to reach anybody there by phone, nor had Mick been able to contact any former staff members other than the housekeeper.

A weathered sign that read BELLEFLEUR appeared at the foot of a driveway to my right. The tall iron gates were closed and padlocked. Across from them was a grove of pepper trees; I parked there and crossed to peer through the gates. There wasn't much to see: a deeply rutted asphalt driveway, untamed trees and shrubbery, a couple of out-buildings that even from a distance looked to be in poor repair. Far down the driveway a steep slate roof missing many slabs protruded through the foliage, but from this angle I couldn't make out the main house.

I went back to my car and took note of my bearings. About a hundred yards from here the road looped in a large U and doubled back to the freeway and, fortunately for me, it passed by the Hoffman estate—the home of my former client. If I was in luck, I might be able to access the Bellefleur property from there.

It struck me as an odd coincidence, but peculiar coincidences happen, or there wouldn't be a word for them. And, for whatever reason, they abound in investigative work. This was one of the largest and most beneficial I'd experienced lately.

5:45 p.m.

The gates of the Hoffman estate stood open. As I drove in I spotted Suzy Cushing, the great-niece of Jane Hoffman, my former client, as well as a linguistics major with an emphasis on geopolitical physics at Stanford. Her job was to live with and look after her great-aunt, as well as to oversee the affairs of her great-uncle Van, who was currently—and probably forever—institutionalized.

There'd been talk that Suzy had been given a minor fortune to care for her aunt Jane when her great-uncle was put away, which wasn't true. All the assets, what there were of them, were in a trust; her aunt's lawyer, not Suzy, was its administrator. And Suzy's caretaking job wasn't any easier than it was lucrative. Aunt Jane had turned into an unpleasant, querulous old woman, forever making demands and complaining when they weren't met according to her exacting standards. However, when she wasn't in classes or studying, Suzy, a gardening enthusiast, spent most of her spare time on the grounds surrounding the house or the greenhouse behind it. Today I found her out front digging in a bed that I recalled had contained spring flowers.

She stood up as I stopped the car. Her short blonde hair was tousled and there was a smear of dirt on her forehead. When I got out of my car and she recognized me, a smile transformed her small, perky face and she jumped up and down like a cheerleader. "Texas cute," Mick would call her.

"Shar!"

"Hi, Suzy. Good work on the house."

Up close, the old two-story French chateau style looked much better than the last time I'd seen it. A fresh, although thinly applied, coat of cream paint and new green shutters perked it up, and Suzy's plantings would eventually round out the pleasant picture.

She hugged me, shedding soil on my clothing. When she realized what she'd done, she tried to wipe it off, but I waved her away. "It's great to see you!" she said.

"You too. How are you?"

"Pretty good. You?"

"About the same. And your aunt Jane?"

"Some days good, some days not so good. But she's still a bitch. I'll be moving her to a nursing home in a few days, and I doubt she'll ever leave there."

"And your uncle Van?"

"He died last summer."

"Oh? I didn't see an obituary for him."

"There wasn't one. I didn't think it was proper, given his criminal past. At the end he was crazy as a bedbug. Whenever I'd go to see him in the nuthouse, he'd just sit there, and then all of a sudden he'd ask when we were going to South America."

"And you'd say?"

"'We're waiting on the money.'"

Hoffman had been an embezzler, but now the money he'd stolen was back where it belonged. However, some strange quirk in his brain had insisted the money was still his, since he was the one who'd taken it.

Suzy said, "I'm so sorry about what happened to your father. I read about it in the paper, and I've been meaning to call. How is he?"

"Mending nicely, thanks."

"Has whoever beat him been caught yet?"

"Not yet, but we're getting close. As a matter of fact, that's why I'm here. A neighbor of yours may be involved."

"Really? Who?"

"Rolle Ferguson."

"Oh, shit. Let's sit down."

We went to the front steps and planted ourselves side by side.

"How well do you know Rolle?" I asked.

"Not very. Just that he's an asshole bigot with too much money, and a rabble-rouser. Always protesting things like gay marriage and civil rights issues. When he was in high school, he picketed the senior prom because the king and queen were an interracial couple."

"Yes, I know."

Suzy picked up a little stick and began pushing it through

the dirt at her feet. "When I think of him at all—which I try not to—I have this theory that he doesn't really care about anything except calling attention to himself, making waves. A crazy megalomaniac in training."

"So it wouldn't surprise you if he's involved in the white supremacist movement?"

"No. Nothing he does would surprise me."

"Does the name Jerzy Capp mean anything to you?"

"No. Who's he?

"A cohort of Rolle's, a racist thug. It's possible Rolle may be bankrolling him."

"Uh-huh. Just the kind he'd hook up with. You think he and this Jerzy are the ones who attacked your father?"

"Looks that way. We just have to prove it. Do you know if Rolle spends much time at Bellefleur?"

"He didn't after his parents were killed, but he's been around recently."

"Alone or with others?"

"With a bunch of guys the last time I saw him. Creepy types just like him."

"When was that?"

"A couple of weeks ago."

"But they could have been back since without you noticing?"

"Oh, sure. If they didn't make a lot of noise."

"What were they doing over there?"

"Partying, it sounded like. All night long. Why they'd want to party over there is beyond me. The place is a wreck—was starting to be even before Rolle's parents died. The Fergusons weren't what you'd call homebodies."

"How do you know it's a wreck?"

Suzy flushed. "You know how you can get an urge to explore odd places? Well, I had one after Rolle and his weird friends left."

"So you went exploring at Bellefleur."

"I did." She spread her hands wide. "What can I say? I'm just naturally nosy."

"Nosy is a quality that's always worked for me. So what did you find?"

"That the property is in even worse shape than I expected."

"Did you go into the house?"

"No way. It was locked up tight and I wasn't about to break in. Trespassing on the grounds is illegal enough."

A wind had whipped up, rattling the leaves of the eucalypti that flanked the house on two sides. Suzy shivered.

I said, "How did you get over there? Climb the front gate?"

"No. A tree growing on our side of the boundary line."

"Mind showing it to me?"

"Thinking of doing some exploring of your own, Shar?"

"Yep."

The tree, a large heritage oak, was at the back of the deep rear yard. Its sturdy, moss-covered branches topped a high stone wall between the two properties by a good dozen feet.

Suzy said, "Put your foot into that notch there, and pull yourself onto the second-highest branch next to it. That'll give you a look into the yard."

I stretched out my foot toward the notch, anchored myself, and climbed.

The land on the Bellefleur side was so overgrown with trees and vegetation gone wild that at first I couldn't make out anything. Then something grayish white fluttered in the breeze, and I focused on it. A badly shredded net, below it the faded green pavement of a tennis court. When I leaned forward and to one side, I had a glimpse of part of the slate roof in the distance.

After a moment I climbed down and asked Suzy, "Can you give me the general lay of the land over there?"

"Sure. If you go in by the main gate, you'll see this ugly mermaid statue, straight ahead is an ugly decrepit fountain. There's a grove of bay laurel trees to the left, a falling-down gazebo to the right, and next to it a collapsed wishing well. From the well you have a good look at the house. There're some outbuildings—a garage, a caretaker's cottage, a potting shed, another shed that was probably where yard furniture and lawn equipment were stored. Driveway's mostly graveled and not well graded. Also long. You want to look out for ruts."

"Why would Rolle want to keep the property when it's in such disrepair? Acreage that size would be a developer's dream."

"That I don't know. I guess a lot of us have hang-ups about our home places." For a moment she looked pensive, then shrugged the mood off. "Want me to come with you?"

"No. Better on my own."

"Well, be careful. I almost concussed myself on a tree branch when I was over there."

"I will. But do me a favor? Call me at this number"—I scribbled it on the back of one of my cards—"if anybody should happen to show up at the front gate."

4:40 p.m.

I climbed the oak tree again. When I was a kid I used to scale trees in the canyon behind our old house in San Diego all the time. But I wasn't so nimble any more; my right foot slipped on the slick moss and for a moment I hung suspended by my left arm. Or maybe by the left sleeve of my sweater. I could feel threads unraveling. Shit! This investigation was sure playing hell with my clothes…

Finally I regained my footing, swung over the wall, and climbed down onto Bellefleur land. Took a moment to orient myself, then walked slowly in the direction of the main gate.

There was the mermaid statue Suzy had mentioned, and was it ever ugly! A product of the early nineteen hundreds, probably shipped from Europe at great expense. Rich people did that kind of thing back then—trying to emulate William Randolph Hearst and his excesses in furnishing his castle down south at San Simeon.

Unfortunately the mermaid had been badly sited and it leaned—sort of like the Millennium Tower high-rise in the city that had gradually begun sinking in recent years. More than four hundred San Franciscans were now stuck with millions of dollars' worth of condominiums that might at any time be sucked into the muck and mire of the Bay.

Turn right, Suzy had told me. I was to look out for ruts— and there were plenty of them. I passed the copse of bay laurel trees and was briefly so distracted by their strong, curry-like fragrance that I tripped over an exposed tree root and nearly fell.

Pay attention, you fool!

I could see the outlines of the collapsed wishing well now, although if Suzy hadn't told me what it was, I would have dismissed it as a pile of long-discarded lumber. And then the fountain…

It was three tiered and even uglier than the mermaid. Carved on the bottom tier were large fish with vicious-looking teeth; on the middle tier gargoyles grinned, their huge, gaping mouths poised to pour water into the surrounding bowl. And on the top tier little naked angels capered—what was their job? To pee on the gargoyles? Of course the fountain was dry, dead leaves and branches skittering through its pillars and pond.

Who, I wondered, had commissioned the construction of this monstrosity? It was old, its marble chipped and discolored, heaps of dirt and debris drifting against its walls. How long had it been since water bubbled and cascaded into the bowl? And why all this neglect, if Rolle was intent on keeping the property?

The gazebo appeared to the right. Part of its roof had collapsed, and weathered ornate trim and latticework were scattered on the ground. The pillars that had held the roof were splayed out around its ruins, as if they all had fallen at the same time. A putrid odor emanated from the wreckage; something had died there not long ago. I skirted it quickly, and when I passed through a tangle of shrubbery I had a more or less clear view of the house.

Massive, three storied, with many wings and a stained, cracked white façade through which orange bricks showed. Hanging shutters, shingles from the roof strewn on the ground. Half-dead yew trees leaning against the walls, brown shrubs that looked as if they'd succumbed years ago. Nothing healthy growing except weeds where a lawn once might have been.

Again the question occurred to me: why the neglect?

I moved to the front of the house, then made my way along its right side. Doors and windows were all securely locked. Through one dirty windowpane into what might have been the living room or parlor, I could make out a grand piano, its lid lying beside it, most of the ivory torn off. I tested the latch. It was locked.

Well, McCone? You've already committed criminal trespass. Do you want to add breaking and entering to the list?

My vibrating cell phone saved me from having to make a decision. I tensed, thinking it might be Suzy reporting someone's arrival. But no, it was Ted.

"Where are you?" He sounded distressed.

"On the Peninsula, at the Ferguson property."

"You better get back here right away."

"Why? Has something happened?"

"Yeah. A car bombing."

Jesus! "Whose car? Where? When?"

"Julia's. Right in front of the building. Less than five minutes ago. The fire department hasn't even got here yet."

"Was she hurt?"

"No, she wasn't in the car. Whoever did it didn't mean to kill her. Must've been set off by remote control. But she's badly shook up."

"I'm on my way."

5:11 p.m.

The news made me mad as hell. The destruction of Julia's ancient Mazda had to be related to the racist attacks, not a coincidental prank by one of the city's "imps," as they liked to call themselves—idiots with an insatiable desire for attention. No, this was a vicious act indirectly aimed at me, Julia's vehicle targeted because she was my employee and a member of a minority group.

A warning to M&R: *Stop investigating us, or worse will happen to you.*

I hurried back to the stone boundary wall as quickly as I could, climbed up and over. Fortunately, Suzy had gone inside the house for some reason, so I didn't have to take the time to say goodbye to her. In the car, as I drove out to the road, I put on my Bluetooth and called M&R's security chief, Bud Johansen. I asked him to post extra guards on the hospitality suite where Saskia, Emi, and Ma were staying, and also to cover the homes of our other employees and warn those who didn't have cars to use WeDriveU for their transportation until further notice. Then I thought of Will Camphouse, and gave Bud his cell number so he could warn him. The alert Hy had put out at the time of the invasion of our home not only covered Avila Street but the Tufa Lake ranch house and Touchstone, so all three properties were already well covered.

As I headed north on 280, I turned the car radio on and punched the channel buttons, looking for a news broadcast that would tell me about the car bombing. Only music: pop, rap, classical, hip-hop. When you wanted music, the news was always blaring in your ears. When you wanted news…

I drove as quickly as traffic would allow. When I arrived at the M&R building, I found the street clogged with a pair of fire trucks, a TV mobile unit and camera crew, and the usual assorted group of onlookers. A tow truck was removing the burned-out hulk of Julia's Mazda. She stood on the curb watching them, gave the car a sad little wave as the truck lumbered off, its flatbed swaying. I parked in the vacated space and hurried to her.

Tears stained her cheeks. This was the first time I'd seen her cry. She put her arms around me and her head on my shoulder.

"Oh, Shar, what am I gonna do? My sister needs the car to take Tonio to school and do the shopping. I need it to work my cases. Why do these things always happen to *me*?"

Julia had had a rough time in the worst part of the Mission district—a life laced with drug use and prostitution—until the birth of her son Tonio six years ago, when she'd determinedly turned her life around.

"You didn't do anything," I said, smoothing her wet hair back from her cheek. "The bombing was aimed at me, and I'm pretty sure I know who did it."

"You do? Who?"

"The same bastards who attacked my father."

"*Dios mío!*"

We went inside, the night security man waving us through. His eyes were kind as he said, "So sorry, Ms. Julia."

"Thank you, Roy."

In the elevator I said to Julia, "I'll get somebody to arrange for a rental car for you."

"Thank you, but I can't take advantage—"

"Your car was destroyed while you were on the job. M&R owes you a rental."

"I think I have enough saved up for a new used car. That one was becoming unreliable."

"Then start checking the automobile ads. If you need help, I'm sure the agency can float you a loan."

We found a handful of people waiting with Ted and Mick—SFFD and SFPD investigators with questions about the bombing. I dealt with them as quickly as I could, then took Ted and Mick aside to make sure Elwood and Ma and Saskia and Emi were all still safe and sound.

"No problems on that front," Mick said.

"And on other fronts?"

"A lot of messages have been piling up for Ripinsky, but he's unreachable."

"Closeted with security people, maybe, or in transit."

"Aren't you worried about him?" Ted asked.

"I've been a lot more worried about him in the past. Anything new on Rolle Ferguson and Jerzy Capp?"

"No," Mick said. "Whatever their agenda is, they seem very good at hiding it. But Derek's still working on it."

"Okay."

"I take it you didn't find out anything at the Ferguson place in Atherton?"

"Not much. I wasn't there long enough." I told him about what I'd seen there and what Suzy had told me about Rolle.

"Pretty much tallies with what I've been able to find out," he said. "Do you want me to summarize all this and e-mail the report to Sergeant Anders?"

"Good idea. She's swamped with work, but I want to keep her in the loop."

"She'll get the news about this car bombing through departmental channels, but I'll mention it too. Do you suppose it's connected with Ferguson and Capp?"

"I'd be surprised if it wasn't."

"What're you going to do now?"

"Catch up on some routine stuff."

"I'll be doing the same at home. Call me there if you need anything."

6:35 p.m.

The offices had gradually quieted down, except for the clicking of computer keyboards in a couple of cubicles. The phones had ceased ringing.

I'd thought I needed some time to myself, but now felt restless, totally out of sorts, as I often did while waiting for something to happen. Pacing around my office did nothing to calm me. In fact, all it got me was a broken fingernail from smacking my hand on a file cabinet. I repaired it and sat at my desk until the polish dried, gazing at a nearby bookcase. My eyes settled on the latest edition of *Hints on Criminal Investigation*, a twenty-pound tome that had been more or less my Bible since I'd started in the business. I took it down, cradled it in my arms, and curled up in the armchair under Mr. T., the schefflera plant.

I wasn't looking for anything specific—the book contained nothing I didn't already know—but paging through it might set free an idea that would steer me onto a different track. I was rapidly coming to think of the present one as nonproductive.

Practically since the first day I could read I've had a habit of poring over heavy volumes such as *Hints* and the California penal code. Not because what they contained had anything to do with my world; at seven years old, I was just curious, and the weighty books felt good in my small hands. But I ask you, how many seven-year-olds know that it's illegal to trap birds in a public cemetery? Or that animals are barred from mating publicly within 1,500 feet of a tavern, school, or place of worship? Or that it's unlawful to let a dog pursue a bear or bobcat at any time?

Tell that to the animal kingdom.

As I sat there, paging through the tome, the phone rang. Saskia and Robin and Will had heard about the car bombing and called earlier with a flurry of concerned questions. Now it was Elwood, who had been in physical therapy most of the afternoon. I did my best to reassure him, but he still sounded worried when we ended the call.

I was about to pack it in and go home when a call came in from Sergeant Priscilla Anders. She sounded tired and discouraged. "I haven't made any headway on your father's case, Ms. McCone. And they're piling the workload so high over here that I'm about to collapse under it. And now this car bombing…"

"My nephew, Mick Savage, is going to e-mail you the details of our agency's investigation, bring you up to date on what we've found out."

"If I'm lucky I'll get to it by a week from next Tuesday."

I knew the kind of burnout that was getting to her. My former operative Adah Joslyn had experienced it at the SFPD before she came to work for me. Now she and her husband, Craig Morland—once with the FBI—had recently formed their own agency and were enjoying a more low-key life.

I said to Anders, "Mick'll send the file anyway. No hurry on reading it." But I knew she would read it tonight. That's the kind of cop she was.

Hy remained incommunicado. The offices grew chilly—my fault for decreeing that we must conserve energy. I decided to read *Hints* at home in the comfort of my warm bed.

But on the way down to the garage, where I'd moved my car after the tow truck departed, something interesting occurred to me. I sat down on the elevator floor, propping its door open, and again began leafing through the pages of the heavy volume. Something I'd read earlier had jogged my memory.

8:55 p.m.

I finally found it, on page two hundred under the heading "Criminal Techniques."

```
A common tactic among criminals seeking to avoid
detection is MISDIRECTION. Let this be a warning
to neophyte investigators that very often in a
case, the scenario of a crime, whether generated
by oneself or the suspect(s), is not always as
it seems. Criminals will often prepare a story
backed up by a few convincing facts. Others will
construct elaborate tales whose vast details
will require a great deal of time and effort
to untangle. Evaluate those acts and details
```

carefully. Inconsistencies may appear among them
that will set you on the road to a solution.

Well, I knew all that, but reading it set down in such a matter-of-fact manner reinforced my past experiences. So who, if anyone, had misdirected me recently? Dean Abbot? He'd been deceptive from the first, and there was little doubt in my mind that he was mixed up with Ferguson and Capp. Maybe I hadn't been watching the currents that eddied around me as carefully as I should have. Dozens of people had gained my trust over the years, and there was no guarantee that one of them hadn't turned on me. Or that someone who had nursed a strong but well-concealed grudge hadn't finally acted on it, as had been the case with the man who'd torched my house on Church Street.

No, I *hadn't* been careful enough; in this business you need to harbor a good measure of paranoia, but I'd become lax in that department. Complacency, owing to my relatively comfortable and peaceable life, had set in. Time to fan the flames of paranoia and let it take over.

Sure. How about Elwood had orchestrated his own attack for some incomprehensible reason? (Utterly ridiculous notion.) Or maybe Julia had firebombed her own car for the insurance money. Or Suzy was another racist in cahoots with Rolle Ferguson. Or Will Camphouse had had ulterior motives in coming here. Hell, maybe Chef D was trying to poison me with his pasta al Cubano—it *had* made my stomach hurt.

Stop! This is the way to madness.

Footsteps on the concrete stairs beyond the open elevator door. I jumped as Will's voice called out to me.

9:10 p.m.

Well, think of the devil and he may appear. But if Will was a devil, he was an exceptionally cheerful one. "Hey," he said, "I've just come from the hospital. Elwood's doing okay. But he was semidelirious and mumbling a lot of mismatched things that didn't make much sense taken separately or together."

"What things?"

"'Expansion' was one. Another was 'Stomp foot.'"

"Applicable to the attack, I suppose."

"Another was 'Special ops.' Funny, because he was never in the military."

"What else?"

"'Cuff.' 'Crystal.' Something that sounded like 'Too many dials.' Something about no hair. Any of it mean anything to you?"

"The attackers may have been bald? I'd better go talk to him myself and see if I can make any sense out of that jumble."

"You can't, not until tomorrow. They sedated him for the night right before I left."

"Damn!" I stood up. "Let's get out of here, Will."

"Sure. Want to go get a drink?"

"Yeah. There's a place near my house. We'll ditch our cars and walk over."

"I gotcha."

"Oh, Will, wait. How did you know I was here?"

"That new receptionist in your office...Jason?"

"Jason Lieberman."

"Right. He figured you'd be someplace between the elevators and your car, since he didn't hear it leave."

Jason had a keen ear and might make a damn fine operative sometime in the future.

10:39 p.m.

Jasmine's Lounge reminded me of Ellen T's, my long-vanished watering hole across the way from my long-vanished apartment on Guerrero Street in the Mission. Ellen's had been a homey place, chock-full of healthy plants and happy customers, Ellen herself a blowsy, overweight woman who was intent on convincing her customers—even the workmen who preferred drinking and playing pool in the back room—to eat often and sensibly. Years later the earth-mother bartender had disappeared from San Francisco. I'd tried to locate her, but I was caught up in my burgeoning career by then, and I hadn't tried very hard.

Will and I squeezed into one of the smaller booths near the rear of Jasmine's long space; philodendron branches spiraled down toward us from hanging baskets. He looked around, narrowing his eyes as he studied the crowd pressing close to the bar up front.

"What do you see?" I asked.

"Millennials who are as dumb as I was in my Gen-X stage. Hopefully they'll outgrow it before something bad happens to them."

"Such as?"

He sighed. "The usual things that afflict most generations: drug addiction, alcoholism, homelessness, joblessness, inability to afford an education. Bad marriages, financial failures, incorrigible children, incarceration. They seem handsome and prosperous and happy tonight, but somewhere in the future there's a slippery slope waiting for most of them."

"My, aren't you the cheery conversationalist tonight."

"Sorry. It's survivor's guilt creeping out."

"Why now?

"I don't know. Maybe it's just my age. I had a very sheltered life growing up. My father was a university professor, my mother a poet… Well, you know that. There was always enough money for anything reasonable. I got a good education, a good job right out of college. None of this living on hardscrabble land and having to beg Indian Affairs for everything I needed. Now I realize I got off easy. But I also realize that my job's trivial compared to what other Natives are doing for our people, and as a result the folks I meet when I go to the reserve are wary of me."

"Maybe you should have a heart-to-heart talk with Saskia. She seems to have a good grasp of cultural conflicts such as yours."

"Have you ever talked to her about yours?"

"A few times. When I first found out about my heritage, I was devastated—not by who I was, but because of the lies that had been told to me. But I'd always felt different—as if I was straddling two worlds but didn't understand why—so it was easier to make my peace with the people who were misguidedly trying to protect me."

"Protect you from yourself?"

Unwilling to talk about it any more, I bared my teeth at him. "I'm a very dangerous woman."

He held up his hands in mock horror. "I won't cross you."

"Okay," I said after our drinks had been served, "suppose we discuss what's on my mind right now: misdirection."

"Misdirection?"

I quoted the gist of what I'd read in *Hints*. "Why does that seem relevant to this whole megillah?"

Will laughed.

"What?" I asked.

"A Shoshone who grew up thinking she was white with a touch of the Indian paintbrush speaking Yiddish slang."

I laughed too. "So I'm multicultural. Anyway, misdirection. Are all these threatening acts that seem to be directed at me and my family just the usual racist crap? Or are they designed to mask another motive?"

"Such as what?"

"Good question. One I can't answer."

He said, "This misdirection—is it deliberately created by the people you're investigating? Or is it inadvertently created by the investigator?"

"You mean are they steering me wrong, or are my preconceptions steering me wrong?"

"Either."

"Or maybe it's a combination of the two?"

"I've thought of that. Let's consider the ad biz: the client wants one message to get across to one customer base; you want to broaden the market for their product. So you alter their message, but not enough to upset them. And they alter your alteration, but not enough to reject your ideas. And then you bring in another alteration that basically is what you proposed in the first place. You've got them confused, but suddenly they like the concept. And then you've got a successful campaign."

I considered what he'd said. "Now I think *you've* misdirected me."

"That was my aim." He yawned loudly and stood up. "Sleep on it, symbolic cousin."

We held hands as we weaved along to my place.

11:57 p.m.

I slipped into the dream as easily as I would have into the pilot's seat of our Cessna, then sped in the wrong direction on a runway that seemed to go on endlessly. And when the plane started bumping the way they do when they're ready to fly, I decreased rather than increased the throttle and had to pull off and taxi around again.

When I was finally airborne after a clumsy takeoff, a heavy mist enveloped the plane. I scanned the ground for landmarks, kept an eye out for approaching aircraft, but the mist was impenetrable. The radio did me no good: all the towers and UNICOM stations within range were dead silent.

The words of my now-deceased flight instructor, Matty Wildress, echoed in my mind:

Always have a landing place fully fixed in your head, and consider alternatives as well. Accidents can happen. They will *happen. Planning and forward thinking can save your life.*

Well, Matty, that's all fine and good, but what am I supposed to do when the weather and all systems fail me?

They won't.

Oh yeah?

Because there's another system that you've got going for yourself. One you failed to mention.

What system?

Your instincts. Use them!

I used them and not only landed the Cessna unscathed, but returned from the dream to my own bed.

Now, what the hell did all that mean? I wondered, propping my head up on my pillow.

More psychic hints pushing me toward the concept of misdirection. In the dream I'd been fooled by my instincts and the lack of the landmarks we use to set our VFR courses. Also fooled by the lack of chatter from a control tower or UNICOM.

Envelopment in mist: flying blind. Necessary to get my vision back.

Matty's message: it's all instinctual.

Yes, right. Three truths to think about, here in the midnight darkness.

WEDNESDAY, DECEMBER 27

10:19 a.m.

Elwood wasn't fully awake when I tiptoed into his room, although the nurse had told me he soon would be. "Yesterday he took to raising his bed and waiting for his meals," she said. "Then he eats like he hasn't been fed for a week. And then he's ready for another. Remarkable."

Even more so, I thought, considering he's eating hospital food.

She left me, probably to hurry along the food cart, and I sat down and listened to his rhythmic breathing. Such a strong man—I was grateful to him for passing on his genes to me. I'd been stabbed, shot, put into a coma, nearly drowned, and almost killed in a plane crash, but had eventually emerged from those situations reasonably unharmed.

I sat there listening to the early-morning hospital sounds: the scurrying of rubber-soled shoes, greetings and faint laughter from the nursing station, carts being wheeled back and forth, pagers and heart monitors beeping. All of this brought back memories that weren't unpleasant in retrospect. I'd been reassured and well cared for on my long road to recovery.

Elwood mumbled something. I strained to hear, but he didn't repeat it. I moved my chair closer to the bed and murmured his name.

"Wah…wah…wah…"

Nonsense syllables.

"Watch!" he said suddenly, emphatically.

Another silence. Was he waking up or just dreaming? After half a minute or so: "Daughter…"

At least half-awake, I thought. "I'm right here."

"Blue green."

"I don't understand."

"Cuff. No hair."

"Who has no hair? One of the men who attacked you?"

More silence. His face twitched as if in frustration.

"What are you trying to tell me, Father?"

"Cuff…"

"Cuff?"

"Titanium. Expansion. Stomp…foot."

Titanium?

"Too many dials."

"What kind of dials?"

"Stomp foot. Crystal."

I waited, but he didn't say anything more. "Too many dials," I prompted. "Stomp foot. Crystal."

Still no response.

I tried the other phrase he'd spoken to Will Camphouse. "Special ops."

Again no response. He'd fallen asleep.

I remained by his bed for quite a while, hoping he'd wake up. But he didn't.

11:20 a.m.

The offices were quiet when I arrived, everyone going about their middle-of-the-week business. I waved to Jason Lieberman and Kendra, who were conferring at the reception desk, and went directly to my office. Then I sat down and tried to put meaning to my father's seemingly meaningless mumblings.

Expansion.
Titanium.
Too many dials.
Blue green.
No hair.
Special ops.
Cuff.
Stomp foot.
Crystal.

An odd assortment of words and phrases. He'd said them to both Will and me, so they must connect somehow, have some meaning. But no matter how hard I tried, I couldn't fit them together so they made any sense.

I gave it up for the time being, swiveled around, and booted up my computer.

Only nothing happened. The screen stayed dark.

"Come on, you wretched machine," I said aloud and tried again. Still nothing. "Don't tell me you've died," I told it. "You're top of the line, almost new. You can't give up on me."

A hubbub started in the hallway, people scurrying around. Seconds later Ted rushed in.

"Your computer working?" he said.

"No. What's going on?"

"Nothing good."

Now I heard excited voices babbling. Derek, Julia, the entire staff. And Mick, shouting, "Calm down! Everybody calm down!"

Now I was alarmed too. "What the hell's going on?" I asked Ted.

"Don't know. Try powering up again."

Still nothing.

"Damn!" Ted said. "Major problem here—"

Derek burst in without bothering to knock. "We've been hacked," he said angrily. "Malware's locked up all of M&R's computers. Not just here, across the nation; I just took a call from New York. Mick's checking with the branch offices in other countries. They're bound to have been affected too."

"But why, for God's sake?"

Mick entered my office. "That's not clear yet, but whoever did it has some kind of agenda. Remember the Russian hackers and how they affected the last election? Whoever infected us with this virus has skills equal to theirs to get past the firewalls we installed. Probably used some sort of sophisticated pop-up device, or an e-mail that somebody in one of our offices opened, thinking it was genuine."

"So what do we do about it? Call the cops?"

Mick snorted. "They couldn't figure out what the problem is, much less solve it. We've got to contact the feds—Homeland Security, it's their jurisdiction because of the threat to government systems. They—"

He broke off because now something else was happening. My computer was still switched on, and the screen suddenly lit up. Almost immediately I heard the familiar bonking noise that indicated an incoming message. I clicked the e-mail icon and the message appeared.

TO: Sharon McCone/personal & confidential

RE: Your files

They are locked. We will restore your acess to them when you agree with our terms. If you do not agree, we will step up our personal attacks on you, your family, and your asociates. We guaranty that at least one of these new attacks will be fatal.

$3,000,000 from your personal and corporate accounts you will wire-transfer to a bank of our choice in the Cayman Islands no later then 6:00 PST tomorrow. Instructions will follow.

WE WILL BE WATCHING YOU. OUR SPIES ARE EVERYWHERE.

Do not claim you cannot acess and give us this sum. We know the exact amount and location of your asets. Do not contact the police or feds. Do not try to trace this message, it will be beyond your capabilities. If you do not do exactly as we tell you, we will shut down negotiations and immediately give retaliation. FATAL RETALIATION.

Instructions for the wire transfer will be our final communication. Once we have received the $3,000,000, you will never hear from us again.

I gripped the arms of my chair, so furious I felt like screaming. I had to force myself to speak in a seminormal voice. "So that's what that son of a bitch Rolle really wants. Money."

"But why?" Mick asked. "He's got plenty of his own."

"Not three million in ready, tax-free cash."

"Yeah, but are we sure he's the one behind this?"

"Who the hell else?"

"Dean Abbot. If he was capable of breaching the security system on your house, he's capable of shutting us down."

"He may be a computer genius," I said, "but I don't see him devising a crazy scheme like this. He's a follower, not a leader. And he's not stupid or semiliterate. Read that extortion demand again. Unoriginal, trite, like something out of a bad TV movie. Words misused, misspelled. Just the sort of thing an out-of-control nutcase like Rolle Ferguson would dream up and write."

A pause as Mick reread the message. "Yeah, I see what you mean. Can we raise that much?"

I calculated. "Not unless we want to go into chapter eleven. It's an impossible amount. And we're sure as hell not going to pay."

"So we should let Homeland Security handle it?"

"Not entirely. Derek, you get in touch with them, tell them we'll cooperate fully. Mick, round up everybody for a staff meeting in the conference room."

After I'd finished telling everybody what had happened and what we were up against, I asked Roberta to check out the Divisidero Street condo on the chance that the bunch was holed up there now. Then I spoke with a Homeland Security agent Derek had on the phone. And then I took Mick aside.

"I'm going out," I said. "Keep things here as organized as you can."

"Where're you going?"

"After Dean Abbot."

"Not alone, Shar. He's likely to be dangerous. Let me come along as backup."

"No, I need you here."

"Derek, then—"

"Dammit, no! Just do what I told you. And don't worry, I won't take any unnecessary risks."

"Famous last words."

Mick meant well, but I was tired of people, especially men, being so solicitous of me. Was my age showing? Did I seem feeble? Forgetful? Unsure? I didn't feel that way. I didn't look that way either—not unless I had a very defective mirror. But sometimes I was afraid I was joining the ranks of women— and men too, I supposed—whom no one actually *saw* any more.

3:50 p.m.

Clouds were drifting in toward Piedmont from the north, indicating that the predicted storm or at least heavy fog were soon to follow. The little house on the hilltop looked battened down for the duration of the bad weather, but lights in the back of the first floor indicated someone was there. I rang the bell, keeping my finger on the buzzer longer than was necessary. My other hand was inside my purse, curled around the handle of the .38.

Heavy footsteps approached, the door opened partway, and Quentin Zane looked out.

"You again!" he exclaimed.

"Me again. Is Dean here?"

"No."

"I need to talk to him right away. Where is he?"

"I don't know. He left early last night and he hasn't come back."

"Did he take a computer with him?"

"He had his laptop case, yes. And an overnight bag."

"He didn't give you any idea where he was going?"

"No."

"You'd better not be lying to me, Quentin. Your roommate is involved in a scheme that can do harm to a number of highly placed individuals. If you're in on it too, you're looking at prison time."

Quentin's face turned white. "No! I didn't have anything to do with the whole ugly thing."

"But you know about it."

"Go away, leave me alone."

He started to close the door, but I stuck my foot in the way and then pushed inside. He backpedaled, his eyes wide and scared. "You can't come in here—"

"I'm already in."

I shut the door, looked around. The room was spacious, with yards and yards of white carpet that looked to be of good quality. On it sat an assortment of furnishings that reminded me of what young, affluent people had aspired to in the late twentieth century: Danish modern or Norwegian woods or Swedish something-of-that-sort; spoon-shaped chairs that swiveled and rocked; an orange-patterned couch that I knew would be impossibly hard because it had no springs, just a wooden platform with cushions tossed on top. And on the walls, framed displays consisting of collages of *New Yorker* covers. For a person who was supposed to be on the cutting edge of high tech, Dean Abbot was as retro as they come.

I said, "You know what Dean's mixed up in, Quentin. Don't try to deny it."

"I'm not a racist."

"No?"

"No. I swear I'm not. I grew up in a home where *nigger* and *wop* and *chink* and *dirty Jap* were common household terms. For a long time I didn't realize there was anything wrong with them, but in fifth grade I called a little first-grade girl I liked a nigger, and she started crying, and my teacher set me straight. I never used any of those ugly words again. Or any of the ugly words men use against women."

"Good for you, if you're telling the truth."

"I am, honest I am."

"Dean *is* a racist, one of the worst kind."

"I know that now," Quentin said woefully. "I didn't until after he moved in here; letting him in was the biggest mistake of my life."

"You never read his blog?"

"No. I don't read or create blogs. I *work* in the computer field, but that doesn't mean I want to spend all my time at a keyboard."

"All right. Dean breached the security system on my house. You know that too, don't you?"

"I…"

"Sure you do. How did you find out?"

He shook his head.

I took a step toward him. When I'm angry I can be menacing, even to the toughest of people. And the one I was dealing with here could charitably be called a wimp.

"Answer the question, dammit!" I demanded. "How did you find out?"

"I…I overheard you and Dean talking when you were here before. I asked him if it was true what you'd accused him of, and he admitted it. He…he even bragged about it. And then he told me to lie about it if you came back."

"What else did he tell you?"

"Just that he and some friends of his were going to make a lot of money and use it to finance some plan they had, he wouldn't say what the plan was. He tried to talk me into joining up with them, but I refused. I didn't—don't—want any part of something like that."

"He didn't say how they were planning to get the money?"

"No."

"Or who these friends were?"

"No."

"Why didn't you report all this to the authorities?"

"Dean told me to keep my mouth shut or the same thing would happen to me that happened to your father." Quentin's already piteous expression crumpled, and for a moment I thought he might start to cry. "If he finds out I talked to you—"

"He won't find it out from me."

"I'm afraid of him and those friends of his, Ms. McCone. You should be too."

"Wrong. They should be afraid of *me*."

Quentin blinked at my response. To take advantage of his confusion, I said, "Before I leave, I want to take a look at Dean's office or workstation."

"Oh no. I couldn't let you do that!"

"Who owns the house or is primary on the lease?"

"I own it."

"Then you can allow me to check things out. It's legal. I'm an investigator in the employ of a prominent criminal defense attorney."

As it had many times before, the ploy worked. Quentin didn't even ask who the attorney was; I would have given him Glenn Solomon's name and number if he had. He just gestured in a distracted manner and said, "All right, I'll show you."

4:25 p.m.

The house had four bedrooms. The two at the rear, one with a deck that overlooked an untended backyard, were Abbot's bedroom and office, connected by a full bathroom. Quentin followed me while I searched for anything that might tell me where I could find Rolle Ferguson and Jerzy Capp.

The office first. Computer equipment—a large Dell PC; small and large scanners; two Epson printers. The computer would be password protected, naturally. There was no point in asking Quentin if he could gain access to any of them; as skilled a hacker as Abbot was, he'd make sure no one could get into his files, especially his roommate. There were no paper files in the desk or workstation, nothing that even hinted at a connection with Rolle Ferguson, much less his present whereabouts.

The bedroom held no leads either. All it told me was that

Abbot was fairly neat, had lousy taste in clothes, and didn't use prescription drugs or the illegal kind.

When I was done and went back into the hall, Quentin said nervously, "*Please* leave now, Ms. McCone. If Dean comes back and finds you here, he'll be furious."

"You're really afraid of him, aren't you?"

He looked away.

"Well, you needn't worry. I doubt he intends to come back for a while, if at all."

"What...what makes you think that?"

"Call it an educated guess."

"But what if you're wrong?"

"I'm not."

He wrung his hands. "Oh, God, I don't know what to do..."

"You've got three choices," I said. "Move out of your own house for the time being and hole up someplace. Or if you're really desperate, call one of those twenty-four-hour locksmiths and get all the locks changed, then consult with a lawyer and have him file a restraining order."

"What's the third choice?"

"Hope I find him and his racist buddies soon and have the lot of them locked up in jail where they belong."

5:40 p.m.

On my way to the Bay Bridge I put on my Bluetooth and clicked on Mick's cell number. He answered right away. I told him about my talk with Quentin Zane, the futile search of Abbot's quarters.

"Did Roberta turn up anything about Ferguson and his bunch at the Divisidero condo?" I asked.

"No. The place is still closed up tight, neighbors haven't seen any sign of them. You coming back here now?"

I couldn't return to M&R and wait around doing nothing. Action was what I needed, now more than ever. Bellefleur was the only place I could think of where Ferguson and Capp and Abbot might be, or if not, where I might find something that would lead me to them.

"No. Atherton."

"Shar, for God's sake, don't go down there alone, especially not tonight. There's a big storm coming in—"

I knew that. I had checked aviation weather that morning, as I often do even when I'm not flying. "Don't try to talk me out of it."

"Hy would if he were here."

"But he isn't, is he?" The words came out harshly, and I realized I was angry at my husband, angry at Mick and most people I knew.

"Shar, please—"

I turned the phone off.

Why so much anger? I asked myself. The attack on Elwood, the other racist outrages against me and my family, the hacking shutdown and the extortion demands...all of that, yes, sure. But there was another reason too.

I was tired of dealing with stupid crimes.

Extortion and blackmail. Kidnapping. Bank robbery. Embezzlement. Spousal and child abuse.

When you think about it, all crimes are stupid.

More people get away with murder than you'd suppose, but those are usually cases where the cops aren't sure if it is murder or not. Child and spousal and elder abuse—they're in the same category as murder. A lot of abusers get off because the victim refuses to testify against them, but as a society we've become more aware, lessened the stigma of being a victim, as we have with rape. As for extortion and blackmail, they wouldn't exist if the victims refused to comply with the criminals' demands.

Refused, like we were doing.

But what about kidnapping?

Now that was a tricky one. The risk to the victim's life was an emotional powerhouse. But a fair amount of kidnappings are shams, or the victim is dead before the ransom demand has been made.

Bank robbery? How many retired bank robbers did I know?

Well, one, actually. Big, tough guy. Got caught, served his sentence. Tried to write a book, but he was semiliterate because he'd been too busy planning heists to pay attention in school. Finally he went to live with his sister—and ended up working as her gardener for minimum wage.

I was approaching the Bay Bridge now. I stopped playing pointless mind games and concentrated on my driving.

6:30 p.m.

The rain—not too heavy yet—had started by the time I reached the exit for Atherton. A thick overcast hung low over the Peninsula hills, making the night very dark. Visibility was poor. The narrow road I was following looked different than it had in the daylight and kept confronting me with curves and switchbacks that I didn't remember. I couldn't make out any lights in the big houses that I knew stood beyond the wind-whipped branches of the trees that surrounded them.

I tuned into a weather report on the car radio. This storm was going to be a biggie, the meteorologist said, coming down in icy blasts from Alaska. Travelers' advisories were in force: stay off the roads. As I switched off the radio a downpour hit, pelting my car brutally. I could barely see the road, and my tires were slinging up mud against the undercarriage. I crept along and finally came to a wide place off the pavement and pulled into it. It wasn't as large as I'd thought, and my car's nose plowed into a thick stand of brush on the other side. The car stalled, and I turned its lights out, deciding this was as good a place as any to wait out the onslaught.

I sat still for a few moments, gathering my wits, which seemed widely scattered, then reached for my phone. But a banging sound made me fumble it, and pellets began to bounce off the hood.

Hail! What more would this horrible night bring?

More hail, descending harder. Larger pellets, and a freezing cold that penetrated the metal cocoon around me. I recovered my cell, but reception was spotty here. Finally, after several dropped connections, I reached into the cramped space behind the seat and pulled out a heavy blanket I kept there. It was zipped into a plastic cover, and at first my fingertips were too numb to open it. Once I did, I swaddled myself in it head to toe.

Dammit, the car needed a new paint job, but I'd planned on having it done in the spring. But with the cracks the hail was probably opening up, I'd better get to the repairs quickly before the salt air from the Bay irreparably corroded the body.

7:10 p.m.

Finally the hail stopped and the rain abated somewhat. I started the car. At first I feared I'd be mired in the thick mud, but I eased out gently and breathed a sigh of relief when I was on the road and once again on my way to Bellefleur.

Downed trees—mostly the fragile eucalypti—were confined to the brush to either side of the road. Branches of all sizes were strewn everywhere, making it difficult to navigate. Dripping water from the thick pine branches made it seem as though it were still raining heavily, and wind continued to rock the car.

At a place where the road split into two lanes around a huge, ancient sequoia tree, I paused again to consider my options. I could park somewhere near the entrance to Bellefleur, well out of sight, and try climbing the gate. But it was topped with spikes, and I doubted I could see enough of the house from the road to tell if it was occupied. Gaining access to the estate's grounds would be easier and safer via the oak tree on the Hoffman property.

As I passed the gates to Bellefleur I slowed down and peered through its bars. Right. I couldn't tell if there were any lights in the house. I went on to the Hoffmans'.

The gate there was open, as it had been on my last visit, and I drove through and up the drive. The house was completely dark except for amber nightlights. Nobody home. Suzy had said something about taking her aunt to a care facility, I remembered. Had that been scheduled for today?

I parked to the far side of the driveway, where the car would be partially obscured by the shadow of one of the eucalyptus trees. The rain had dwindled to a drizzle, but if the National Weather Service reports were accurate, this was only the calm before the biggie.

I had a sudden desire to give up this quest. Go to a phone booth—if I could even find one of the nearly extinct devices—and call the San Mateo County Sheriff's Office. Turn it over to them. Go home. Lie in a warm bathtub for twenty-four hours. Sleep in my own bed for a week.

Sure. You never have abandoned something like this. You never will.

I locked my purse inside the car, after removing my gun and the small, powerful pen flashlight I carried. Then, with the .38 in the pocket of my jacket, I zipped up and angled through the side yard to the stone boundary wall.

Climbing the oak tree was much more difficult in the rainy dark. My foot slipped as I eased out onto the branch above the wall, and I nearly fell before regaining my balance. When I'd crawled out far enough that I feared the branch might break, I dropped down, my rain boots sinking deep into mud. They made a sucking sound when I pulled them out.

I drew the hood of my parka up, but it seemed to have lost its waterproofing. Cold rain from the trees' leaves rolled down my face as I made my way, the shielded beam of the penlight guiding me, through the shrubbery and bay laurel, the untended grass and tall weeds. Then, through the rain, I saw the main house looming ahead.

It was dark, and there were no vehicles, no signs of life anywhere in the vicinity.

On my earlier surveillance, I'd noticed that one of the windows near the rear corner of the house had a hole in it. I made my way there and held the light up close to the glass, moving it around so I could see inside. The glass was dirty, but I could make out that the room beyond was a kitchen.

The inside catch was fastened, but the hole was down near the sash.

The cracks were spidery, with some of the glass missing, small pieces and larger ones starting to separate from the frame. I used the butt of my .38 to break out a few shards and widen the hole. Then I lifted the sash and climbed inside.

The kitchen was cold and musty. Once inside I flashed the light around to orient myself. The kitchen was old, evidently never remodeled: kitschy brown-and-yellow tiles with gingerbread men on them; black-and-white checkerboard floor. The paint on the yellow cabinets was peeling, and a few of their doors were missing. Inside one I could see a massive flour sifter, in another a set of canisters enameled in a plaid tartan pattern. The sink was porcelain with a drain board and a number of chips; the stove was a gas model probably dating back to the 1950s. The refrigerator—of the same era—was working but contained nothing but a jar of Skippy peanut butter.

Scattered about on the countertops were pizza boxes, Chinese takeout cartons, crumpled beer cans, and liquor bottles. A trash can overflowed with more beer cans and bags from fast-food outlets. The typical detritus of people who didn't care about their surroundings.

I followed my light's beam into the other downstairs rooms. It looked as though vandals had been at work in them: the damaged piano, smashed gilt-framed mirrors, ripped and slashed silk upholstery on the sofas, little side chairs with their legs broken off. The huge dining room table had scar lines as if someone had tried to ice-skate on it. I hated to think what I'd find upstairs.

Again I wondered why Rolle would have allowed such a valuable asset to deteriorate so badly. Or did someone besides him have control of the estate? Maybe our information was flawed; that could happen in the area of estates, trusts, and the like.

A marble-floored staircase that I could swear I'd seen in dozens of B movies curved to the second story from the tiled foyer. I moved up it, feeling the give of the risers and banister. Dry rot. A fixable problem, but costly, and the owner would have to care...

The faded red carpet of the second-floor hallway was threadbare. The walls were covered with similarly faded wallpaper in a maroon fleur-de-lis pattern that must have dated back to the sixties. Doors spread out along a gallery to either side of the staircase, some open, some slightly ajar. In spite of the empty silence, I kept a tight grip on the .38 as I moved along, nudging at each door until I could see the room beyond. Most were empty—stripped by vandals, I supposed. Two doors were closed.

I took hold of one of the knobs and eased the door open. The room here looked as if someone had been living in it: rumpled blankets and sheets and pillows on the double brass bed. A coverlet hung off onto the floor on one side. I checked the closet, found jeans and shirts and underwear in a heap on its floor. Men's clothing: medium-size denim shirt; jeans, size thirty-six by thirty-eight; size thirty-six briefs. Smaller than the average man, as Rolle's description and the photographs Mick had turned up indicated.

I checked the pockets of the shirt and jeans. Nothing in the shirt. Small change in the jeans, as well as an unused matchbook from the Twenty-Second Century. Circumstantial evidence at best; Charley Willingham hadn't identified Rolle as one of the rowdy group in the bar the night of Elwood's beating, and Rolle could have picked it up at any time.

A bureau stretched along the wall that backed on the gallery. Its drawers were full of more clothing, same sizes. A smaller central drawer had evidently been used as a catchall: scissors; baggies of extra buttons; souvenir key chains; obsolete tie tacks; a pair of those air freshener balls that are supposed to take the stink out of your athletic shoes; two Bic pens, both dry. The key chains were from standard places: Disneyland, Cal Expo, Marine World—probably childhood acquisitions. A key—a big old-fashioned gold-plated one— had been pushed to the rear, probably forgotten.

I took it out and examined it, then looked at the doorplate. A key to a room in this house, perhaps?

A second door led to a shared bathroom, a common feature in houses of this vintage. My flash showed blue-and-white tiles on the walls and floor: a whimsical Dutch pattern of windmills. The windmill pattern was repeated in the borders of the white window curtains.

I looked into the medicine chest above the pedestal sink.

Pills. A lot of pills, most of their bottles without labels. The two with labels—benperidol and fluphenazine—showed Rolle's name; the bottles were nearly full, their date from two years earlier.

Psychotropic drugs. I knew because at one time or other they'd both been prescribed for my half brother Darcy. They were used to treat aggressive and antisocial behavior, depression, and certain forms of psychosis. Rolle had been off his meds for quite a while.

I went out onto the gallery, looked along it at the closed door at its far end. When I tried the knob, it wouldn't budge. I inserted the key I'd found. The lock clicked, the door swung inward.

There was something very wrong in this room. The windows were open in spite of the rain. Their curtains billowed out, their windmill borders dripping. The sink in the attached bathroom also dripped, but old fixtures often did. The stall shower curtain—more windmills—fluttered, but only at one end, as if the other was being held down with a heavy weight. My scalp rippled unpleasantly as I pulled the curtain away.

Crumpled in the far corner was the motionless figure of a man.

I stepped closer, bent down. The man's eyes were wide open, staring at nothing but the dullness of death. His lean, middle-aged face was covered with blood-caked cuts and bruises, and blood spotted the front of his shirt. He'd been beaten to death.

I didn't have to wonder why. He was Hispanic, might possibly have had Indian blood judging from his cheekbones and the jut of his nose.

Now Rolle and his racist gang had crossed the line into murder.

There was no identification in the victim's jeans or shirt; I steeled myself long enough to check the pockets. Who was he? Not a homeless person—his clothing was old but clean, his hands calloused but free of dirt, and his fingernails trimmed. A person they'd kidnapped somewhere and brought here to torture?

Whoever he was, he hadn't been dead long, probably less than two days. There was no odor yet, just the scent of rain. Rolle's troops hadn't bothered to bury the body, but were they crazy enough to just leave it here to decay? I didn't think so. Wherever they'd gone, they intended to come back and dispose of it.

I closed the curtain and left the room without touching anything else. What I needed to do now was get out of this house and off Bellefleur as quickly as I could. Once I was back on the Hoffman property, I'd call the San Mateo County Sheriff's Office and report what I'd found. I'd have to admit committing a felony trespass, but given the circumstances, I doubted I'd be charged for it. And then I'd notify Mick and Sergeant Anders, if I could get hold of her.

That was the plan, but things didn't work out that way.

I retraced my route to the gallery, and was halfway down the stairs when I heard the gates clang and saw lights flash beyond the rain-streaked foyer windows. Headlights, two sets of them.

Shit! Rolle and his band were back.

I could hear the cars now as they roared up in front and stopped. The only thing I could do was run back upstairs and away from the head of the stairs. I stood tensed in the shadows along the wall. If they came up here, I'd have to find a place to hide quickly, in one of the unused rooms.

Car doors slammed. Loud voices punctuated by laughter sounded before and after they trooped inside. There must have been half a dozen of them, all talking at once. I recognized one of the voices: Dean Abbot.

Another one said, "Okay, now we celebrate."

"What about the spic?"

"No hurry. We'll take him out later and bury him someplace."

Somebody else said, "Jerz, you shouldn't've offed him. He was only looking for a gardening job."

"Shut up about that. So I lost my cool, so what? One less spic in the world."

"Suppose somebody knows he was gonna come here?"

"How? We got rid of his truck, didn't we?"

"Why didn't you just leave him in it? Or stuff him in one of the outbuildings?"

"Oh, quit your whining and let's crack those brewskis and do some coke. It's party time."

Party time! My God, partying with a battered corpse upstairs in the bathroom. What kind of people were we harboring in our society, so full of hate, so lacking in empathy, so soulless? I couldn't even imagine what it would be like to live in their skins.

Heavy footsteps as they trooped out of the foyer. Heading for the kitchen, I thought. There hadn't been any beer in the refrigerator, so they must've brought it with them.

My first thought was to tiptoe down the stairs, get out through the front door. But the dry-rotted steps creaked and the kitchen wasn't far away. If they heard me, they'd all come in a rush. I couldn't hope to hold them at bay with my .38, or shoot them all if they attacked me. And some of them might be armed too. The smart thing was to stay concealed until the law could be gotten out here.

I went down the hall, away from the kitchen, into one of the empty rooms, leaving the door slightly ajar. Then I took out my cell with the intention of calling Mick, having him contact the San Mateo County Sheriff's Office.

But my luck was really running bad tonight. The signal was weak, and all I got when I tapped out his number was static. I tried again, over by the window. Same thing.

Now I had no choice but to wait for the bunch of them to leave or else find a safe means of escape.

But meanwhile there might be something more proactive to do, rather than simply hide. I left the room, walked softly back along the gallery to another that I calculated was above the kitchen. Inside, I located the heat register. It was open, probably had been frozen that way for years. There'd be one in the kitchen too, and from long experience with old houses, I knew that open registers acted as intercoms.

When I knelt down and put my ear close to this one, I could hear their loud voices. They were almost as distinct as if the gang had been in the room with me.

Unfamiliar voice: "Man, you guys sure lucked into a good thing when you jumped that old Indian. Who'd've thought he was the father of that bitch Sharon McCone."

"Wasn't luck." Jerzy's voice. "I knew who he was and I'd been following him for two days."

"Why?"

"Because I wanted to hurt the bitch where she lives. She

sent a buddy of mine to San Quentin a few years ago. Ever since then I been reading about her and that Ripinsky and all the other lives they've ruined. Was time to take action. Too bad you weren't with us that night, Rolle."

"I wish I had been. But beating up Indians and spics is minor league, like all those protest rallies. Now we're headed for the big time."

"I'm not so sure a full-scale race war's a good idea, at least not right away. Look what happened to Charlie Manson and his big plans."

"Manson was an idiot. All that shit about his people living in some hole in the ground until all the niggers and spics had done each other in and then crawling out and taking over the world—that was just plain crazy."

"Right. You ask me, all he wanted was to get laid and have his girls do murders for him."

"Point is, you have to have long-range planning and plenty of money. Then you can recruit an army, gather enough ordnance to start things rolling."

"We'll have plenty of cash pretty soon if the McCone bitch forks over the three mil."

"She will. What choice does she have? Dean saw to that."

"Yeah, he did. Even if he did get caught hiding in a broom closet."

Laughter.

"But what if they call in the feds in spite of the warning? The government's computer people can reverse the lockdown."

"Not right away. It'd take time, right, Dean?"

"The way I set it up, it will."

"So if they don't pay the three mil by six o'clock tomorrow

night, we carry out our threat. Off one of their employees. The spic girl, the one whose car we blew up, or the Jap or the fag office manager. They'll pay up then, damn quick."

I clamped my teeth so tightly together pain shot through my jaw. The sick, cold-blooded bastards! Standing around sucking down beer and snorting coke, and calmly talking about murdering Julia or Derek or Ted if they didn't get their goddamn three million dollars.

"A killing means even stronger heat from the feds." Dean Abbot.

"So what, as long as we collect?"

"McCone already knows who I am, figures I'm the one hacked her home security system."

"Don't sweat it, Dean. If they ever do make the connection with us, we'll be forted up in some new digs by then. And before we go, I'm gonna burn this place to the ground. I hate it that much."

Where did they plan to go? Some desert hidey-hole like the Manson Family had in Death Valley? I hoped one of them would say or drop a hint, but none did. They went on to discuss the kind of ordnance they'd need to accumulate, then clinked bottles in a toast—

"Here's to the revolution!"

"And white power!"

11:35 p.m.

The luminous dial of my watch told me it was almost tomorrow. I unfastened it and put it in my pocket. Just as I did that, the gang began trooping out of the kitchen without saying where they were headed. Coming upstairs to fetch the dead gardener for burial?

I got to my feet, went to stand tensed and listening by the door with my fingers tight around the handle of the 38. No sounds came from the stairs, or anywhere else I could make out. Minutes passed in silence. They were still somewhere in the house; I would have heard them if they'd left. But where?

Easing the door open, I stepped out onto the gallery and over to the head of the stairs. Then I could hear rap music and their muted, drunken voices and hoots of laughter, coming from the other end of the house. Still partying. In a room where more coke had been stashed, probably.

I couldn't stand to stay here any longer. It was icy cold in the house—probably no central heating, and Rolle and the rest so fueled by alcohol and drugs that they didn't need it—and my joints had begun to ache. With the racists clustered at a distance, I might never have a better chance to sneak out than right now.

Slowly I started down the stairs, pausing on each riser to listen. The creaking and groaning of the old wood that came with each step seemed loud in my ears, but either the sounds of my exit didn't carry or the thugs were making too much noise to hear them. Their whooping celebration continued unabated.

I finally reached the bottom of the stairs, tiptoed across the foyer to the front door. I held my breath as I turned the knob, but Rolle hadn't bothered to lock it. I eased it open, slipped through, closed it quietly behind me. And then I was out into the chill, wet night.

Rain was falling again, driven by gusts of wind. The night had grown colder. The storm front would bring more heavy downpours before too much longer. I had to get out of here before that happened. But navigating the grounds in the dark would be far more difficult than coming in had been. I didn't dare use my flashlight until I was well out of sight of the house.

Light coming through blurred windows at the house's far end helped guide me past the parked cars and across the muddy, rain-puddled driveway. Ahead, the darkness was thickly clotted. I couldn't even make out the outlines of the massive fountain.

I dodged through dripping vegetation and around the wishing well. The gazebo was wrapped in shadow, but the faint putrid smell remained in spite of the rain, warning me away. Another victim of Jerzy's savagery? No. Judging from what I'd overheard, the Hispanic gardener had been the first. Probably what was in the gazebo was just a small animal that had crawled inside the gazebo and died there.

I groped my way toward the fountain and the copse of bay laurel trees beyond. As I neared the fountain, I pivoted to look behind me at the house. A vine or something snagged my foot, sent me sprawling headlong into a trough of mud. Something that turned out to be a fallen tree limb stopped my forward slide—with a sharp blow to my forehead that jarred the .38 out of my hand.

I pushed up on hands and knees, shaking my head to clear it, and fumbled around until I found the gun. Extricating myself from the mud was a struggle. It clung like Gorilla Glue.

Jesus, it was as if this place were trying to claim me! People had described the Wellands, the supposedly haunted estate on the nearby road, in those terms. At the time I'd heard the rumors, I assumed that those spreading them were aficionados of such films as *House on Haunted Hill*, but now I could feel the grasping pull of Bellefleur. A place without ghosts, but made evil by the man who now owned it and his followers.

I managed to stand up, then to wipe as much ooze as I could off the .38 before stuffing it into my jacket pocket. The rain and wind had slackened again, a lull before the main force of the storm hit. I looked toward the house. All that was visible of it from here was parts of the darkened second floor and roof. I could use the flashlight now if I kept the beam shielded with my hand—

What was that?

Sounds behind me, faint but unmistakable—somebody moving over the muddy ground in my direction.

Sounds of pursuit that the rain had kept me from hearing before.

I strained to see through the darkness. Couldn't pinpoint the exact source of the sounds, but could tell that they were coming closer. Dammit, I must have been seen leaving the house or crossing the driveway.

But it didn't sound like more than one man out there. One of them must have left the others for some reason, maybe to go out to the cars for something. Whichever of the bastards, he was too drunk or too sure of himself to have raised an alarm—thank God for that. And that he didn't have a flashlight with him. But did he have a weapon?

No sense in trying to outrun or outmaneuver him in this swampy darkness. I couldn't let him catch me, but neither did I want to ambush and shoot him unless it was absolutely necessary; the sound of even one shot was liable to alert the others. Hide, then, at least temporarily. If he gave up the chase and went back to the house, it might give me just enough time to get to the stone boundary wall and over it to my car.

The nearest place of concealment was the fountain, its massive hulk looming off to my right. There must be plenty of places to hide among the three ornate tiers—among the large fish with their vicious-looking teeth, the grinning gargoyles, or even the capering angels.

I made my way to its near side, trying to be as quiet as I could, and crouched in the shadows to listen. My fingers around the handle of the .38 were numb from the cold, but that wouldn't keep me from using it if I could. If it would fire after being immersed in water and mud.

Now I could no longer hear the sounds of pursuit. Had he stopped too? Yes, but not for long. Then I heard him again—close, so close I had a glimpse of his dark shape. He must have heard me in spite of my caution, he must know where I was headed.

I had just enough time to climb over the fountain's wall, flatten myself against the side of its puddled basin, before he came stumbling up not a dozen feet away.

"You can't get away from me, bitch," he called, the words slurred by all the beer he'd drunk, and harsh with the arrogance that had sent him chasing after me alone. "Come on outta there."

Jerzy Capp.

The deadliest of the bunch, with blood already on his hands.

"You hear me? I know you're in there."

Had he seen me slither inside? Or he was he just guessing?

"Make me come in there after you, you'll regret it. I'll beat the living shit out of you."

He must not be armed. If he were, he'd have said so instead of making the beating threat.

Misdirection.

There were pebbles on the basin floor, I could feel them underfoot. I reached down, gathered up a handful, and flung them toward the copse of bay laurel.

Capp's shadowy shape whirled toward the trees. I used the opportunity to boost myself up between two of the nasty-looking fish. One of their sharp marble teeth opened a gash in my cheek.

But Capp hadn't been fooled, damn him. He turned back toward the fountain, barking a harsh laugh.

"All right, you asked for it. I'm coming in."

I waited, perfectly still, not even wiping off the blood that was trickling down my neck. His head appeared over the lip of the basin, then he clambered over and I heard him drop down and start groping around near the center column.

He said in a nasty drunken singsong, "Come out, come out, wherever you are."

I'd been holding my breath, but I couldn't hold it indefinitely. I tried to exhale and then inhale without making a sound, but his hearing must have been acute. He let loose an animallike growl and started pawing the column right below me.

I couldn't remain silent any longer. "Stay back," I snapped. "I've got a gun."

"Bullshit."

"I'm warning you, Jerzy—"

"Oh, so you know who I am, huh?"

"I'll shoot if you come any closer."

"Like hell you will."

He lunged upward, caught hold of my leg, and tried to drag me down toward him. I clung tightly to one of the stone fish with my left arm, trying and failing to kick free.

He fumbled for a grip on my other leg. I could have shot him then, or tried to, but I was still afraid of the noise carrying to the house. Even high, Rolle and the rest would know a gunshot when they heard one. Instead I reversed the .38 and smashed the butt against the hand clutching at my ankle.

He yowled in pain and let go. I pulled both legs up and back, then pistoned them toward where I thought his head was. Lucky aim in the darkness: the heels of my boots caught him smack in the middle of his forehead.

The impact knocked him backward onto the floor of the bowl. His grunting cry of pain was cut off by a loud cracking sound. The back of his head slamming into the concrete?

I stayed where I was between the two marble fish, holding the .38 as steady as I could, but there were no more sounds from Capp. No reaction from the house at all.

The pain in my cheek throbbed, and a new, stabbing one radiated from my ribs. I breathed shallowly for a bit until it eased some, then exchanged the gun for the flashlight in my coat pocket. I switched it on, aimed the thin beam downward.

The sound I'd heard had been Capp's head hitting the concrete. He lay crumpled and unmoving, his eyes half-open and shining in the light. I couldn't tell if he was dead or alive, and I didn't care. All that mattered right now was that he wouldn't be chasing me any more.

I turned off the flashlight, climbed out of the fountain. There was no sign of anybody else in the darkness; the rest of them were still partying back at the house and had the music up to a high decibel level, probably hadn't even missed Capp. Once I got into the bay laurel, I put the flash on again, shielded the beam, and followed it the rest of the way to the boundary wall.

It turned out that I didn't have to waste time trying to charge and use my cell. There was a light on in the Hoffman house now; Suzy was home. Five minutes later I was talking on her phone to the San Mateo County Sheriff's Office.

THURSDAY, DECEMBER 28

7:48 a.m.

I was resting uncomfortably on a plastic chair in a waiting room at the sheriff's substation, a cup of cold coffee on the table beside me. I'd been there all night. My eyes felt as if they'd been rubbed with sandpaper; my clothes were the same filthy ones I'd had on when I fled Bellefleur; my body craved sleep, but I was too agitated to settle down—even if there had been a place to do so.

I couldn't begin to count the number of questions I'd been asked and had answered, over and over again. By the sheriff and his investigators, FBI and Homeland Security agents, Mick and then Ted on the phone. Hy had undoubtedly been subjected to the same, provided they'd been able to locate him. God, I was sick of questions!

Rolle and his followers had been rounded up at Bellefleur by a team of sheriff's deputies acting on a hastily obtained search warrant. They'd still been partying, and too drunk and/or high to put up any resistance. Fortunately, they hadn't bothered to carry out their intention of burying the gardener Jerzy had beaten to death; his body was still in the upstairs bathroom. The deputies had found Jerzy in the

239

fountain where I'd left him, alive but still unconscious, with a cracked skull. He was now in the prison ward at the San Mateo County Hospital.

Dean Abbot's laptop had been found in the house, along with evidence of the gang's racist activities, and was now in the hands of Homeland Security. The HS agent agreed with me that it was the computer that had been used to shut down M&R, and that its hard drive would contain enough data to help their experts restore our operation and eventually convict Abbot of the hacking crimes.

Naturally Rolle and Abbot and the rest had hollered for their attorneys and were refusing to talk to the authorities. They were being held in the county lockup until it could be sorted out which agency had jurisdiction and would take custody of them.

So why did they still need me?

My hackles rose as I saw one of the Homeland agents approaching across the waiting area. I got to my feet and was about to bark a question of my own at him—*Can I go now?*—when he said, "Thanks for your time and your assistance, Ms. McCone. We won't be needing you any longer."

"Well, finally!"

"But please keep yourself available in case we need to confer with you again."

"Confer with me? You mean ask me more questions?"

"If necessary."

"Oh, wonderful. There's nothing I'd like better than having to repeat myself a few hundred times more."

"Excuse me?"

"Never mind. The hell with it."

I turned my back on him and walked out into the new day.

FRIDAY, DECEMBER 29

4:40 p.m.

As soon as I got off the elevator I heard laughter in hospitality suite two. Saskia, Robin, Ma, Emi Nomee, and Will Camphouse—celebrating New Year's early. I'd been on my way home from visiting Elwood in SFG when Saskia called to invite me to the little party they were throwing.

I didn't feel much like celebrating. I hadn't completely recovered from the events at Bellefleur and the all-night interrogation in San Mateo, and Hy still hadn't been located. The visit with Elwood had lifted my spirits somewhat, but he had been given pain medication before I arrived and was a little disoriented, and I hadn't stayed long. The fact that the feds had restored M&R's computer network would have been more cheering if the organization weren't still in a state of upheaval as a result of the shutdown.

But socializing with other family members was better than moping around the office or home alone. So I'd agreed to join them.

Saskia was behind the small bar, mixing margaritas, when I went in. Robin sat on one of the stools chatting with Will and Emi. The only one who didn't seem to be a little tipsy and having a good time was Ma, who sat slumped in a chair looking glum.

"What's the matter with her?" I whispered to Saskia as she handed me a margarita.

"Reality, I believe, has finally caught up with her."

I went over and kissed Ma on the cheek. "Why the long face?"

"It's over with Elwood and me. He told me so this morning."

No, he hadn't. He'd never known anything was *on*. Another fantasy or just plain face saving this time?

"I'm sorry." I covered her hand with my own.

"I'll never love again."

Fantasy. "Sure you will."

"Of course he's still not in his right mind after that beating. I'd be a fool to take up with a man who's...not quite right."

Face saving. "Of course."

She sighed heavily and slipped off the stool. "I don't feel like celebrating. I think I'll go lie down for a while."

I watched her leave. She seemed diminished, frail. It occurred to me that as a family we would need to pay more attention to Ma in the future. Maybe get her some psychological help. But if she'd been living in her fantasy world for so long, as Patsy had said, what was the harm in it? We'd have to have a family meeting about the problem.

Saskia said, "I overheard. She's backpedaling on her story. But the disappointment is only temporary. She'll be all right when she's back in familiar surroundings in Pacific Grove."

Would she? Lord, I hoped so.

SATURDAY, DECEMBER 30

AFTER MIDNIGHT

was dreaming again: Elwood and his mumbled words to Will and then to me.

Expansion.
Too many dials.
Bluish green.
No hair.
Crystal.
Special ops.
Cuff.
Stomp foot.
Titanium.

Over and over and over...

Maybe the reason I couldn't make sense of them, I thought when I awoke in the morning, was that they didn't all fit together into one piece. Maybe the answer was that they had to be considered individually or in separate groups.

11:35 a.m.

Elwood was sitting up in his hospital bed. His color was very good today, his eyes bright, and—another promising sign— he'd been arguing with Dr. Stiles when I arrived about why he couldn't be released into my custody immediately. When the doctor told him that they had to be careful with patients of "a certain age," Elwood's response had been, "Age—bah!" Stiles had looked at me and added pointedly, "Also patients of your daughter's age who have been through a period of emotional turmoil, to whom I'd recommend a complete physical checkup."

"Father," I said now, "have you remembered anything more about the attack?"

"No. It's still a blank."

"Consciously, yes. But subconsciously I think you do re-member."

"Why do you think so?"

"Several things you said to Will Camphouse and to me while semidelirious. Words and phrases."

"Such as?"

"'Expansion,' for one."

He considered. "The Expansion Arts Program in Rhode Island, specializing in psychedelic and deviant art." His eyes twinkled. "The latter is mainly concerned with women's oversized breasts."

"I doubt any of those are relevant. Another word you spoke was 'titanium.'"

"Symbol Ti, atomic number twenty-two."

"How come you remember the periodic table of elements?"

"I studied advanced chemistry in high school, Daughter.

Some things stay with you." He shook his head. "But the important things, they just go as you grow old…"

I let that pass without comment. "Okay, next, 'blue-green.'"

"Your Christmas present, perhaps."

"I received it, and thank you."

"How…?"

"Rae intuited it and gave it to me."

"She's a good girl, that Rae."

"Okay," I said, "let's get back to this: 'Too many dials'?"

He shrugged. "There are all sorts in our world. Old-fashioned phones. That fancy stove you and Hy have that I'm unable to work."

"Special ops?"

Long pause. "Yes. It was the name of the present I was going to buy Hy for Christmas."

"And what was that?

"A Special Ops aviator watch. His is in shoddy condition. In a business such as yours a man needs to be safe."

The watch that Rae had also intuited. Of course! That explained 'titanium' and 'expansion,' and 'too many dials.' Those new aviator watches were made of titanium and had an expansion band and more than one dial.

Elwood went on, "I had concluded that such specialized watches couldn't be bought locally and I would need to order one from a catalog, but I remember looking in the jewelry store window and seeing one on display."

"Just before you were attacked?"

"Yes."

"Was one of the men wearing an expensive watch?"

"Yes." Elwood's eyes brightened; his memory was returning swiftly now. "It was the last thing I saw, beneath the cuff of his shirt sleeve, before I lost consciousness."

"Cuff" explained.

"Did you notice his wrist? Was it hairless by any chance?"

"No, but one of them had a bald head."

"No hair" was explained.

"Were you able to fight back when they started beating you?"

"Very little. I remember stomping on one man's foot. Then as I was falling I managed to smash the dial of his fancy watch against the grate over the store's window. I heard the crystal break."

"Stomp foot" and "crystal" explained. And why he'd said, "too many dials."

So it was Elwood who had inflicted the injury that caused Jerzy to limp at Chef D's. Good for him! Both father and daughter had hurt the bastard.

The smashed crystal was a solid piece of evidence that Jerzy had led the attack against Elwood, provided he hadn't had it repaired. Chances were he hadn't, because he'd been too busy plotting extortion and race war with Rolle Ferguson to take it to a jewelry store.

"Is there anything more you need to know about that night, Daughter?"

"No," I said. "The fact that you've regained your memory is all that matters."

5:55 p.m.

To my relief Hy had finally resurfaced that afternoon, with a long-distance call to me at M&R. We'd spoken only briefly because he was in transit. The hostage situation had been resolved successfully, and he'd be home tonight.

I was curled up on the sofa in front of a crackling fire when I heard him come in. He dropped his travel bag on the floor, crossed the room, picked me up, and held me tight. I clung to him for a long time before he set me down.

"I could use a drink," he said. "How about you?"

"Please."

He went to the kitchen and returned with a bottle of Dry Creek Zin and two glasses, which he proceeded to fill.

"To your homecoming," I said, raising my glass.

He raised his. "To you and the end of that crazy racist business."

We sat close under the green-and-blue Hudson's Bay blanket that we always bring out at the first frost. His hand was warm on my knee.

He said, "How's Elwood? Still doing okay?"

"Thriving, in fact. If he has his way, he'll be out of the hospital and home with us the day after New Year's."

"He really does have amazing recuperative powers for a man his age."

"I hope I've inherited them," I said. "So tell me about the hostage situation."

"Not much to tell. I'll fill you in later. Right now I want to hear the details of what you went through."

He'd monitored the news reports on his laptop while in transit, so he already knew the basics. I provided the details he'd asked for, glossing over some of the more hazardous ones. Finished by using one of his favorite expressions when he'd squeaked out of a difficult situation: "Piece of cake."

He wasn't fooled. "You know, McCone, you take too many

risks sometimes." His face flushed, suffused with emotion. "You need to be more careful in the future. Please."

"So do you."

"Touché. Any new developments?"

I told him what Elwood had remembered about the attack. "I notified Sergeant Anders so she could add aggravated assault charges to Jerzy Capp's list of crimes. She called this afternoon to report that Capp still had the watch and that it hadn't been repaired. With Elwood's testimony, that should be enough to convict him of another hate crime."

"And add a few more years to his prison sentence. What about the gardener Capp murdered? Has he been identified?"

"Yes. Carlos Sanchez. He eked out a living by doing gardening and handyman work."

"Poor guy. He picked the wrong place to look for work."

"That's for sure. The San Mateo DA cut a deal with the feds: they get to prosecute on the murder and accessory charges; Homeland and the FBI will deal with the federal cybercrime."

"Have Ferguson and the others turned on each other yet?"

"Not yet."

"I'll bet some of them do. Rat out their buddies to cop pleas and save their own asses."

"They'll still do jail time."

"A few more bigots off the street—and out of our lives."

"Amen to that."

Hy put a finger to my cheek and ran it down my neck and then to my breast. "Missed you," he said before we kissed.

"Mmmm…"

"We've got to spend more…quality time together."

"Mmmm…"

After an interval—a long interval that alarmed the cats, who fled—we got up and gathered our clothing. Hy picked up the wine bottle and glasses with one big hand.

"Let's continue this…discussion upstairs, McCone."

"An excellent idea."

MONDAY, JANUARY 1

12:01 a.m.

Happy New Year! 'Should auld acquaintance be forgot and never brought to mind…'"

Crystal flutes full of champagne, wine, sparkling water, and—in one case—Dr Pepper were raised in toasts. A bad year had ended. Maybe the new one would be brighter.

Fourteen of us were gathered around the snack-laden table in Hy's and my dining room. Mick. Rae and Ricky. Ted and Neal. Several other friends. John and his new lady, an attractive blonde named Diana. Will. Derek.

The huge glass bowl had been drained twice of what Rae called her "sneaky punch," but it hadn't sneaked up on any of us because we'd been stuffing ourselves with finger food over the past four hours. Chips and dips, pâté and crackers, cheeses and olives and pickles and marinated mushrooms—all had been consumed as if we were a tribe that had been stranded in a desert for weeks. Hot hors d'oeuvres had followed.

Sometimes when I go to supermarkets I feel ashamed. They are so opulent, so crammed full of foods and objects that no human being can possibly *need* but that many of us feel we *must have* that it makes me want to purge my life of them. But I'm as much a product of American society as the next person, and often, as on this New Year's, I plunge in with both hands and a wide-open mouth.

After a while, comfortably stuffed, we repaired to the living room to laze around on the furniture or cushions on the floor before the fire. Conversation was slow and lazy.

I asked Mick, "So how are you and John coming on restoring your house to normal?"

"It's going well. I'm thinking of putting it on the market—too many memories."

It didn't surprise me. "Where'll you go? Back to that little studio where you used to do your computer work?"

"Nah, I gave it up six months ago. There's a condo for sale in John's high-rise. It's small, compact, and all I need."

"Well, if you ever feel the need for wide-open spaces—"

"I know. There's always Touchstone or Hy's ranch. But I'm a city boy and always will be."

Contented silence.

After a while Will said, "I'm thinking of making a change too. Giving notice at the ad agency and then moving here."

I raised my head from Hy's lap. "Leaving Tucson? Why?"

He shrugged. "The work's no longer challenging, seems frivolous. And I like San Francisco."

"What would you do here?"

"Find a position with a small local agency."

"Jobs in the advertising business aren't that easy to come by here."

"I'm not worried. I'll find something."

I had an idea. "You know, the agency's getting too big for me. Hy and I agree that it's not meshing as well with RI as we thought it would. And I'm tired of spending most of my time in my office signing off on reports and invoices and mediating employee spats. I'm an investigator, not an administrator."

"No argument there," Hy said wryly.

"So I could use someone to help pick up some of the slack. How would you like to work for me, Will? Temporarily, if not permanently."

"Are you serious, Shar?"

"Absolutely. As I said, I'm tired of doing administrative work. And you'd be perfect for the job."

"Interesting idea. Let me think about it."

"We'll talk soon. Plenty of time to make up your mind."

We all fell into quiet contemplation.

I thought of Elwood, still in the hospital but more cantankerous every day. Of Ma, whom Robin had driven home to Pacific Grove. Of Saskia, who had returned to her law practice in Boise. Of Emi, winging her way back to Montana because, as she put it, "You can't leave a pothead who calls herself Astral Plane in charge of your business very long." Of Patsy and Ben, whose children had given approval of their marriage plans. Of—

The doorbell rang.

Hy started to get up, but I said, "No. I can't go on being afraid to answer my own door forever."

Still, my palms were damp as I reached for the latch of the judas window.

A young man in a WeDeliver cap said, "Happy New Year!"

I opened the door, saying, "Delivering at this hour is way beyond the call of duty for you."

He handed me the long white box tied with a red ribbon. I dug in my pocket and handed him a generous tip.

"Secret admirer?" Hy said when I brought the box into the living room.

I set the box down and stared at it. "I may be getting paranoid, but what if it explodes?"

"It won't."

"You know who it's from."

He shrugged, smiling.

I opened the box and cleared the tissue paper away. Inside lay a spray of tulips—yellow, white, red, and purple. I sucked in my breath with pleasure and located the card in its little white envelope.

It said: *With all my love, Father.*

Acknowledgments

Lindsey Rose, my editor at Grand Central books, for her patience and excellent suggestions.

Molly Friedrich and Lucy Carson of the Friedrich Agency.

Sarah Andrews, Janet Dawson, Peggy Lucke, Shelley Singer, and Polly Poldowski—my partners in crime.

Bette and JJ Lamb, for making me laugh and forget my troubles.

Laura Neditch, for our Tuesday-morning chats.

Melissa Ward, who tries—against my best efforts—to get me organized.

31901064418892